Honor Bound: A Highland Adventure

by

Laura Strickland

Honor Bound: A Highland Adventure

Cover Art by *Diana Carlile*

The Wild Rose Press, Inc.
PO Box 708
Adams Basin, NY 14410-0708
Visit us at www.thewildrosepress.com

Publishing History
First Tea Rose Edition, 2016
Print ISBN 978-1-5092-0676-6
Digital ISBN 978-1-5092-0677-3

Published in the United States of America

His body stiffened as she eased in beside him, but that did not dissuade her. The rain no longer touched her here and, aye, it did feel warmer.

Ramsay drew a breath even as the heat of his body wrapped around her. She could now catch the scent particular to him—spicy, fresh, and rampantly male, with the tang of Highland air caught in his hair and clothing. Would he push her away?

He sounded amused when he spoke, his voice vibrating deep in her ear. "I suppose this must satisfy some wish you have of lying with your Prince."

It satisfied a wish, right enough, but had nothing to do with Charles Edward. Mara retorted, "My only intention is to lie out of the wet and grow warm. Will you complain about us sharing against the chill?"

"And about having my arms full of bonny lass? Nay."

He thought her bonny. Or did he just tease as he had before? Mara ached to know, and desire rose to her head like a draught of her Da's whisky.

She slewed round in her allotted space until she faced him, her mouth just below his. "I am no' thinking of the Prince," she confessed, "but still how I might thank you properly for your braw gallantry."

"Och, aye?" Did he sound as breathless as she? "And what to your mind would make a proper thank-you?"

Without further words, she pressed her mouth to his. His lips felt warm and surprisingly soft, and their touch sent a spear of need through Mara, blazing in its intensity. Surely she had been born for this, for him.

Praise for Laura Strickland

"The world building is phenomenal."

~Daysie W. at My Book Addiction and More

~*~

"Laura Strickland creates a world that not only draws you in, but she incorporates it…seamlessly…the kind of book that keeps you awake well into the wee hours, and sighing with satisfaction when you've finished the very last page."

~Nicole McCaffrey, author

~*~

"As I read I became so involved with the story, I found it difficult to put down the book.…Definitely…an author to watch."

~Dandelion at Long & Short Reviews

Dedication

In memory of William Ramsay, with affection

Books by Laura Strickland
available from The Wild Rose Press, Inc.

Dead Handsome: A Buffalo Steampunk Adventure
Off Kilter: A Buffalo Steampunk Adventure
Sheer Madness: A Buffalo Steampunk Adventure
~*~

Devil Black
His Wicked Highland Ways
Honor Bound: A Highland Adventure
The White Gull
Forged by Love (sequel to *The White Gull*)
Honor Bound: A Highland Adventure
The Hiring Fair (part of the Help Wanted series)
~*~

The Guardians of Sherwood Trilogy
Daughter of Sherwood
Champion of Sherwood
Lord of Sherwood
~*~

Christmas Short Stories:
Mrs. Claus and the Viking Ship
The Tenth Suitor (also appears in *Brides of Christmas,*
Volume Four)
Valentine Short Story:
Ask Me (part of the Candy Hearts series)

Chapter One

Culloden, Scotland, April 1746

The interior of the small shieling reeked of blood. During the hours just past, that particular odor had been so constant in Diarmad Ramsay's nostrils he marveled that he noticed it now. He had spilled an ocean of blood during the short duration of the recent battle, been splashed with it, had waded through it. The very taste still lingered on his tongue.

But this blood belonged to his father and, by dint of lineage, to Diarmad. Even given all the death he had just witnessed, that made a difference.

He looked at the man stretched hard on a litter hastily constructed from the broadswords and plaids of his clansmen. William Ramsay, a chief of the old order, had always been well loved by his people. He'd devoted himself lifelong to his clan and treated them as might a kindly father, with strength and affection. Eighty clansmen had followed William into this battle; less than half a score now stood gathered on watch around him, both in and outside the half-ruined shieling where they had brought him to die.

Diarmad had no doubt his father did indeed lie dying. All the way up from the battlefield into the hills, pursued by the blighted troops of the English king, William's blood had flowed as from a wellspring; it did still. He could not possibly have much time left.

His clansmen, sober and silent, reflected the truth of that, their faces twisted in grief. The youngest of them, called Arlie, wept openly.

"Where is my son?" The words came from William on a gasp of agony and brought Diarmad to his knees on the filthy floor of the dwelling. His father had taken many a sword stroke during the horror that had been the battle at Culloden. The one that would kill him had rent the Ramsay tartan he wore, and laid open the flesh beneath, right over his great heart.

"Here, Father."

William's eyes—blue-gray as Diarmad's own but now clouded by the onrush of death—turned to find him. One bloodied hand reached out, and Diarmad captured it in both his.

"They'll be coming, William," said Laird Alexander Elliot, who stood behind Diarmad. "We canno' linger."

Diarmad twitched in response. Did the man think they did not know it? Why had he and his entourage accompanied the Ramsay party up out of the carnage? And how dare he take space in this Ramsay guard of honor!

But William's gaze, looking straight past Diarmad, found the man. He asked, "Where is Cainnech?"

Diarmad's heart plummeted, and the pain inside him increased. Even now did his da prefer the company of Diarmad's brother? Did he not see Diarmad, faithful and present, before him? Diarmad fought to rein in his emotions.

As William's elder son, of course Cainnech's welfare would concern him. It concerned Diarmad as well; he had not seen his brother since the height of the battle, when he'd caught a glimpse of Cainnech fighting like a madman, his fair hair flying.

Now he realized with shock that once the last of his father's blood ran out onto the dirt floor of this terrible place, Cainnech would be Chief of their clan—what remained of it.

Hoarsely he said, "Cainnech did not come away out o' yon battle wi' us. We could no' find him."

And did Diarmad's brother—bright, fearless, always ready to laugh—lie beneath the bodies of so many others, their limbs, tartans, and loyalties tangled?

Bitterness rose in him, and he swayed where he knelt. What had they accomplished this dreadful day? What, at such a price?

William's lips moved with difficulty. "We will wait. Cainnech will come."

Elliot spoke again. "William, we canno' afford to wait. We maun carry out the plan."

"How, wi' Cainnech missing?" William cried.

"You ha' another son."

Everyone looked at Diarmad. About damned time someone realized that, he thought, his heart breaking.

Elliot went on, "He looks enough like his brother to carry out the ruse, and being younger may prove a better candidate."

"Carry out what ruse?" No one answered Diarmad, and he tightened his fingers on his father's hand. "Da?"

His father looked at him then, truly focusing this time—seeing him at last. "Diarmad, I ha' a task with which I maun entrust you."

The place of Chief? But that had always been meant for Cainnech. And they did not know for a fact that Cainnech lay dead.

"What is it, Father?"

A cough seized William; bright, foaming blood bubbled over his lips and ran down into his beard.

Tenderly, Diarmad wiped it away, using the end of his own plaid. "Da?"

William looked at Elliot. "Tell him."

"A task was assigned your clan, and your brother in particular," Elliot said, "in the event things went poorly in the battle just past."

Aye, and they could not have gone more poorly, Diarmad thought, his stomach heaving. He looked at Elliot, whose face might be carved from wood in lines of pain.

"The Prince must be got safe away," Elliot went on, "at any cost."

"The Prince *is* safe away," Diarmad pointed out. He had seen Charles Edward at the start of things surrounded by his guards—observing, not risking himself. And when the battle went badly, the Prince had fallen back to a safe distance, while those who stood for him bled and died.

And did, yet.

"The Prince is the Cause," Elliot said. "Without him, there is no hope of regaining the throne."

"There is no hope," Diarmad stated, and some of those gathered around the litter gasped. They had risen to the call of their Chief and their King, pledged their lives, and could not imagine such heresy.

William's fingers grasped Diarmad's, hard. "Whisht, lad! You will not say such things. There is hope while still beats one Highland heart!"

And there in one declaration sounded all the

loyalty of William Ramsay. Even in his agony he held true.

Despairing, Diarmad said starkly, "Many Highland hearts have ceased to beat this day."

Elliot looked at William. "This will not do. He will no' agree."

"He will go as bidden!" William reared up, a lifetime of absolute if kindly command filling his voice. "He is my son."

"We have no' much time," Elliot said again and glanced out through the open door. "We have the guide waiting near Kilmuir."

"Tell him," William bade Elliot once more. "My sons are both men of honor. He will do what is required."

Elliot swept the small room with a glance. "Let us speak alone," he requested of the clansmen.

Reluctantly and in silence they filed from the ruined place, leaving their broken Chief. Diarmad shivered. What could require such a request?

When they had gone and the three of them—Elliot, William, and Diarmad—were alone, Elliot lowered his voice and spoke again. "There was a plan made before the battle, to the benefit of our Prince."

Diarmad searched Elliot's lined face dubiously. "Explain what you do mean."

"We know the Crown will pursue Charles—he is the prize they need to squash the rebellion for good. And so we arranged for decoys, three of them, to play the part of the Prince and hie off all in different directions. No one kens the exact path the true Prince will take, not even me. But before the battle, three men of unimpeachable loyalty agreed to undertake the task of leading pursuers away on these false trails. Your father offered you as one."

"Cainnech," William ground out around his agony. "I thought the honor should go to my firstborn."

"Honor?" Diarmad repeated like a man struck. What honor was there in still more sacrifice? For any such decoy would be dealt with summarily, if caught. "It is mad!"

"To be sure, it is an honor!" William cried. "To serve our Prince and King in any way we can, even to die for the Cause."

Elliot said, "Your brother looks enough like Charles Edward to pass muster at a distance—and you look enough like Cainnech to pass in turn. I and my men will undertake to ferry you by water to Kilmuir where, as I say, a guide has set a route for you northward. But we must leave here at once in order to make the rendezvous."

"I go nowhere! My father is dying."

The words hung in the noisome, close air of the place and defied refute.

"Listen, Diarmad. Listen to me." William's hands clutched both of Diarmad's and drew him nearer the litter. "You must do this for me, so that my honor and the name of our clan may be unblemished. Fighters from the very first we ha' been, and fighters still! With Cainnech gone, you must now carry our standard."

"Cainnech is no' gone." And Diarmad's beloved da did not lie seeping away the last of his blood. Diarmad's world reeled around him so violently he felt the very ground sway.

Pain flickered in William's clouded eyes. "He may be, he may not. In his absence, son, I lay this upon you.

6

I bid you undertake this noble task by my will if not your own."

"Da, please—"

"Heed me, Diarmad! I will have your promise."

William had now grown so weak Diarmad could barely hear the words rasped into the shieling. He wanted with all his heart to say no. How could he vow to continue fighting a Cause in which he could no longer be certain he believed?

But his father's hands compelled him, his father's eyes beseeched and commanded.

William whispered, "'Tis the last thing I will ever ask of you. On your honor, lad!"

Defeated, Diarmad bowed his head.

Chapter Two

Stars patterned the sky overhead, a thousand—nay, ten thousand of them. Diarmad stared upward numbly while he waited for Elliot to finish talking to the party with which they'd just met.

He felt—but nay, he dared not try to describe what lay inside his heart, a gulf of pain so vast his mind flinched from it. *His father was dead.*

Better to concentrate on the stars, on trying to determine where he was besides still ahead of the Crown's soldiers, who pursued any Highlanders fleeing the battle the way hounds chased deer. Their party had crossed the Moray Firth near Allanfearn under cover of night, Diarmad's heart breaking all the while at being denied the privilege of accompanying his father's body home for burial.

Indeed, he could not even tell whether his father's men would successfully escape any pursuers and make it as far as their home lands, far in the north. While he did not doubt the fealty of his fellow clansmen, he believed he should walk at their head and assure that his father would be buried in Ramsay ground, his dust mingled with that of their ancestors.

Instead he found himself at still another shieling, this one burned so recently the smell of destruction hung heavy in the air.

He wanted to get this thing done so he could go

home, lick his wounds, and honor his dead.

"Ramsay?"

Elliot had been addressing him that way ever since they left Culloden, as if Diarmad had become *the* Ramsay at his father's death, entitled to the name. They did not know it for truth, though, and he hoped—prayed—Cainnech lived still.

Elliot approached him with three others in tow. One man, tall and craggy of countenance, might have been of an age with Diarmad's father; the second looked like a warrior, though he now held one arm, roughly bandaged, against his chest. The third wore his plaid up over his hair, half covering his face. Through his numbness, Diarmad felt but a mild stir of curiosity.

"These are the folk, loyal to our Cause, who will see you on your way."

"Graham MacIvor." The tall man put out an arm; Diarmad grasped it. "My son, Robert." The younger man, with the wounded arm, nodded. "My daughter, Mara."

Daughter? She did not step forward but pushed the plaid back from her head so Diarmad could see her better. Starlight illuminated a wide brow, a set of strong features, and a fall of hair that looked wild even in the dim light.

"MacIvor will, as I say, see to the next leg of your journey," Elliot went on. "I maun leave you now. We canno' be seen together again. God keep you, Ramsay, in this undertaking."

Just like that, Elliot stepped away, joined the small party of his men, and disappeared into the darkness.

Diarmad stood alone, in far more ways than the physical.

"'Tis a good, brave thing you do, Ramsay," Graham MacIvor told him. "What think you, Mara? Will he pass for the Prince?"

The young woman stepped forward. "Difficult to tell in this light." Her quick eyes assessed Diarmad in the manner of a trader summing up the qualities of a pony. She lifted a bundle she held in her arms. "We have some fit clothing for you to wear. Once a proper trail is laid, I hope it may suffice."

"Clothing?" Diarmad stiffened. True, he would not find it amiss to get out of these stinking, tattered garments he wore, liberally splashed with blood—much of it his Da's. But he wanted no disguise to make him look like the craven coward who'd fled the field of battle while others stood and died.

"We have managed to locate garments of some quality for you," said MacIvor. "Not so fine, perhaps, as the Prince would truly wear, but they—like you—should pass from a distance. Come and prepare; we canno' remain here long."

With one glance over his shoulder in the direction where Elliot had disappeared, Diarmad followed them. Behind the ruined shieling a fire burned low, casting muted light.

"Let me get a better look at you," the young woman bid Diarmad then. She passed the bundle to her father before setting her hands lightly on Diarmad's shoulders and gazing at him earnestly.

Tall for a woman, she met his eyes almost on a level. He could feel the intensity of her regard as it lingered on his hair, touched his brow, measured nose and chin. He narrowed his gaze and returned her stare with equal interest.

In the firelight he saw her wild mane glowed deep red, her brow white as snow. Impossible to guess the color of those clever eyes, but her nose made a bold statement, and her mouth flirted with stubborn rebellion, though it melted now to unexpected softness.

"Aye, Da, I think he'll do. I am at your service, Laird Ramsay, as at that of the Prince himself." She bowed her head.

Daft wench, Diarmad thought, that she should be still caught in the seduction of Prince and crown. Aye, well, she had not been at Culloden, had not seen what such allegiance bought as its reward.

"Get him rightly clad," MacIvor ordered, "and let us away. We, no more than Laird Elliot, can afford to be found."

He and his son Robert stepped away out of the firelight.

"Strip down," Mara told Diarmad.

"Eh?" He gave her an incredulous stare which she returned with one that flashed like steel.

"'Tis no time for modesty, this. We will be traveling together, and I will likely get more than a glimpse of your hide. Get those things off; we will burn them before the fire dies. I pray these garments fit well enough. We had no' much choice."

Diarmad hesitated but a moment before placing his weapons on the ground, the first part of divestiture. He had lost his dirk somewhere on the battlefield. He suspected it had slipped from his slimy hand after he cut the throat of that snarling opponent who'd tried so hard to take his head. Grief touched him still more strongly. His father had given him that dirk with its antler-horn handle when he turned thirteen. He still had his sword—now nicked by several encounters with bone—and his long knife.

With stiff, wound-hampered fingers, he untied the laces of his ruined sark and drew the tartan from his shoulder. He did not wish for it to lie on the ground.

"You cannot burn this," he told Mara starkly.

"We must. No trace of your true identity can remain."

"Nay; it bears my father's blood."

"Then let him pass into the company of his ancestors, and those stains with him." Her voice sounded neither harsh nor compassionate.

"I will keep this in my pack."

She must have decided not to argue it. He pressed the garment into her hands and drew the remnants of the sark over his head. Beneath it he wore only wounds.

Mara caught her breath. "Those hurts will need to be cleaned and dressed before we carry on. Wait while I fetch some water."

She ducked out of the circle of light, and Diarmad remained where he stood, his numbness increasing.

Surely he dreamed all this—an ugly, lurid dream— and merely lay asleep in his own bed. He would soon awake to find his da still alive and Cainnech coming in with his great smile, teasing him for lying abed so long and demanding he come out to practice at the sword.

The training his brother imparted had stood Diarmad in good stead during the horror just past. By some miracle, he had survived even though so many others had fallen. And he must believe Cainnech, so much the better warrior, had also survived.

"Here now." Mara MacIvor reappeared holding a bucket, cloths, and bandages. "Sit you down."

Again Diarmad obeyed, unthinking and very nearly unfeeling. When he awoke from all this, the promise he'd made his da would evaporate like night with the coming dawn.

"This will sting, my laird. Or should I get in the habit of calling you 'Your Highness'?"

Diarmad made no reply; he sat unmoving as rock beneath her touch, despite the pain. Quickly yet thoroughly she washed him and dressed the worst of his injuries, clucking her tongue from time to time. When she had finished, she ordered, "On your feet now, and off wi' the kilt."

By this time, Diarmad little cared whether she be a young woman or otherwise. He shed the last of his clothing and, half turned away, she urged, "Boots and all. The Prince would not go about in worn deer hide."

When he stood naked in the firelight, she turned back to face him. He once more felt the touch of her gaze—on his chest, measuring the length of his legs and even the manhood between them.

"Aye, you will do," she whispered before she began passing garments into his hands. He donned them as swiftly as possible: fine underdrawers, hose, a clean sark, and boots that barely fit his feet. When she passed him a wad of scarlet wool, he rebelled for the first time.

"What is this?"

"Your kilt."

"It is not." This garment was like nothing Diarmad had ever seen, and glowed warm with the Stuart tartan.

"It is the sort of kilt the Prince would wear. Put it on."

"I will no'."

"You shall," she returned swiftly. "You agreed to

13

this, did you not?"

Unbearable pain flared inside Diarmad, loss so deep it terrified him, accompanied by the reek of blood. So he had.

"Aye, but—"

"Listen to me. If this plan is to succeed, you must become the Prince in thoughts and all."

Diarmad uttered a word he should never speak in the presence of a lady. "In that case, I should hie to freedom whilst others fall dying."

Mara flinched as if he had struck her, but recovered swiftly and stepped up to him. "Where is your loyalty, Ramsay? Where your heart?"

On its way to burial, stretched on a pallet.

He grunted and took the kilt from her hands, only to ask, "How do I don this?"

She put it on him as she might dress a three-year-old child. "This, as well," she insisted then. The fine doublet looked black in the firelight. Diarmad grunted in disgust but struggled into it. MacIvor came up before he finished.

"Well, Daughter?"

Mara stood back, still eyeing Diarmad. "He will serve in appearance, Father. But I ha' my doubts about his heart."

Chapter Three

"I think I should accompany them, Da." Mara's older brother, Robert, spoke vociferously into the half light. "They will stand in need of a guard."

Mara's father pondered it with the fair-mindedness he afforded all important endeavors. "Maybe so, Son, but you are no' the man, and we've no other at hand."

"I am no' the man?" Robert's voice rose in outrage.

"List, Son—your sword arm serves you not at all, now."

"But to let my sister go off wi' a stranger—"

"He has Elliot's approval, and I would trust Alexander Elliot with my very life. And, Son, you and I ha' dead to bury here."

Mara's heart dropped within her like a stone. She barely recognized the remains of her mother and her young sister, both of whom had perished in the fire. If Mara had not gone up over the hill, wanting to see how far off the Sassenach forces lay, she would have been inside the shieling herself when the foray troop happened by.

And she would now be dead, like Ma and Janet.

She tried to imagine her life ending, and failed. What followed death? Nothingness? Heaven? The kirk insisted the righteous found favor at God's right hand.

Must be a crowded tiny bit of heaven, that.

And would God strike her down for such irreverent thoughts? Why would He send her up over the hill and save her, only to strike her down now? Indeed, faith made a complicated proposition.

As did allegiance. She turned her gaze on the man who had been thrust into their midst. He might well be one of the most beautiful men she had ever seen—far handsomer, so she suspected, than the real Charles Edward—but she sensed much wanting in his attitude. True, he had just been through a battle she could only try to imagine, and lost his father. But Mara had lost much also and yet intended to keep her head high and hold to the dream of fealty.

Upon that bright, determined thought intruded another: had Ma and Janet suffered before they died? Had they been taken against their will? Two women alone in a shieling... She had heard such tales before. And impossible to tell now, with their bodies charred to the bone.

Suddenly she wanted nothing so much as to be off and away, even if it was in the company of the disagreeable Ramsay. Nay—His Highness. She must form the habit of addressing him properly.

Pity poor Da and Robert, left to do the burying...

"Mara," Da called, "you must away while still under cover of darkness."

"Aye." She nodded, gathered up her pack, and turned her gaze away from the ruined dwelling. They would not be able to travel far before day broke and they were forced to take cover—likely not far enough to get the smell of burning out of her nostrils.

Ramsay stood looking uncomfortable in his new clothing. Ignoring him, Mara turned to her father and brother.

"Go safely and bravely," Da told her as she pressed into his arms. He held her there a moment, heart to heart. "'Tis a valiant thing you do."

She hugged Robert next and felt him pass his *skean dhu* into her hand. "Here," he said into her ear, "just in case the Ramsay tries to take more than his due."

"You trust no one," she whispered back.

"Aye, and with good reason."

She tried to equate the brother she now held in her arms, stiff and full of pain, with the laughing lad he'd once been. Aye, they were all changed, and not for the better.

"I will get his measure," she told her brother. From the look of the Ramsay's wounds—all of which she'd seen in the firelight—he had fought unsparingly and must, at least, be skilled with the sword.

"See you take care." Robert blessed her with a kiss on the brow and released her.

"Aye, Daughter," her da told her then. "For family and King."

****

The first miles through the dark, filled with brittle silence, set Mara's teeth on edge. She had never been one to chatter constantly and aimlessly like Janet—God rest her blessed soul—but she did like to pass the time, especially when busy at some task or while walking. Ramsay's expression did not encourage conversation though, being closed tight as if his features had turned to stone.

She stole repeated glances at him in the starlight. What features they were! Fine enough, almost, to match that braw body of his. She felt herself grow warm just thinking on it, but that did not keep her from looking again.

He had a noble brow and a proud nose with just a hint of a bow to it that saved him from prettiness. His eyes, a clear blue-gray, might grace any woman. His hair, now tangled and still splashed with blood despite Mara's best efforts, had appeared light brown in the firelight, marked with streaks of red-gold.

She wondered how those wide lips would look if he smiled. Judging by present circumstances, she would not likely find out.

He made no true Charles Edward Stuart, lacking the Prince's warm manner. And she had many a mile to cover with him unless they were caught—in which case they were both very likely doomed to die.

She talked it over in her own head while they moved west and north like hares through the young heather. A troop of the Crown's soldiers could appear at any time. Laird Elliot had told Da they hunted the remnants of the Highland army without mercy. What a pity it would be if she failed to get her false Prince even to his starting point. She twitched her shoulders and looked backward often, sure she felt English eyes boring into her back.

The plan as she understood it was to make some distance before letting those who scoured the Highlands for Charles Edward catch a glimpse of him. Then the chase would begin in earnest. Da had said to pause and let Ramsay rest when the new day dawned. So at last, when the sun began to color the sky in the east and they reached a ruined round tower on a height, she called a halt.

"We had best lay over here," she told Ramsay.

"'Tis getting too light to go on."

He gave her a dour look. "Is the point not that we should be sighted? What sort of foxes are we, that the hounds do not see?"

"Aye, but not yet—not so close to danger. I must get you clear away first. Come inside."

The interior of the tower felt cold and unwelcoming. Littered with rubble from the collapsed roof and portions of a wall, it made no fit place to rest.

Ramsay threw himself down anyway and hauled off his boots. "These accursed things are an abomination," he spat. "I canno' wear them."

"What else will you wear?"

"I would sooner go o'er the heather barefoot." He tossed the highly polished boots into the rubble and scrutinized his feet.

"The Prince would not go barefoot," Mara protested.

"Hang the Prince." Ramsay glared up at her where she stood. "'Tis what will happen to us if we are taken, you ken. We will be hanged."

"Aye so," she sneered, "and is your courage no' up to it?"

"Hanging is an ignoble death with little to recommend it." His gaze moved over her slowly, lingering on her hair, which streamed down over her shoulders. "They will not keep from stretching your neck merely because you are a woman, you ken."

Mara made no reply to that but turned and rid herself of her pack and other burdens. He had offered to help carry nothing all this weary way.

Aye, well, and likely neither would the true Prince.

"This scheme is badly flawed." He spoke bitterly

into her silence.

"You think so?"

"I do."

"Then why did you agree to it?"

That made him shut his lip, and Mara experienced a flash of satisfaction. Had no answer to that, did he, the fool?

"Are you hungry?" she asked after a moment. "I have some food here in my pack."

He shook his head.

"Truly you should eat."

"List, Mistress MacIvor, you may fancy yourself my guide and caretaker, but you are neither. I will eat when I am ready and not before."

"Water?"

He shook his head again.

Fine, then, let him perish of thirst and poisoning from those wounds he carried beneath his finery, as well. She should be outside straining her eyes in the half light, looking for pursuers.

"Tell me more of this ill-fated scheme," he requested. "Where is the sense in us heading away north? Will the Prince not be expected to make for the coast and a ship back to France?"

Mara dug a small measure of food out of her pack. In truth, she felt too sore and sick to eat; every time she remembered what lay back in the burned shieling, her stomach turned.

"The Prince's enemies would like naught better than to have him in their hands. Sure, that would put an end to the uprising for good. But they will no' believe him foolish enough to make straight for France. This scheme has been planned carefully by those far wiser than we. Three teams there are besides that which guides the true Prince, and each given their directions. We were told to head north."

Diarmad leaned back on his elbows and eyed Mara with implacable hostility. "And so you obey like a good, wee hare—no matter that you may run straight into danger?"

"Danger, is it?"

"Aye, so I think."

"We exist only to improve the Prince's chances."

"So our lives mean naught?"

"As compared with his."

"But my life is no' insignificant," he objected. "My father is dead, and my brother may no' have survived the battle. That means I maun take a place at the head of my clan."

Mara said nothing to that, merely eyed him again. Many men such as he had lost their futures and their dreams. Did he think he was the only one?

"Best to get some sleep while you can," she told him. He would be weary from the fight and shattered by what had come after. "I will keep watch and call you when 'tis time to move on."

"So I am to trust you, am I, Mara MacIvor?" He glared full into her eyes. "Faith, I am no' sure I dare."

Chapter Four

A sudden noise roused Mara from her fitful doze. She had patrolled the exterior of the roundhouse for what felt like hours without catching so much as a glimpse of movement on any hand. Then she had come inside and watched the Ramsay sleep for a time, until her own exhaustion caught up with her. Now the bars of sunlight filtering into the interior of the ruined round tower had faded. She struggled to orient herself even as her heart began to pound in her chest. A fine guide she had turned out to be, falling asleep on the very first day of her assignment!

Had they slept the day away? And from whence came the terrible sound that filled her ears and lifted the hair on the back of her neck?

She lay for an instant with eyes wide, examining the emotion that filled her, and those memories upon which it seemed to hinge. *The disastrous battle. The burned shieling. Ma and Janet, dead. The Ramsay.*

By God, that could no' possibly be him making that sound…yet aye, it came from within the tower, and not without.

She sat up in her nest amid the rubble and gazed across the floor to where he lay. The low, agonized moan did indeed issue from his throat, and he thrashed like a child caught in a nightmare.

Dreaming.

Mara caught her breath. Her own sleep had been troubled, full of dark and terrifying images. But what could wring such a sound from a man's throat?

Unthinking, she scrambled over the space that separated them and extended her hand, wishing to comfort yet hesitant to touch him. His new, fine doublet had picked up a layer of dust from their surroundings; his hair fanned out in a wild tangle. His eyes remained tight shut, and his face betrayed the agony of whatever he relived in his mind.

"Nay—nay!" Hoarsely the word burst from him before he fell abruptly silent. Mara stared in dismay. Were those tears on his face?

The Ramsay wept in his sleep.

Her heart plummeted. Ah, she might not like the man—other than to look at. But his pain spoke to that she also felt, and so touched her. Indeed, it must touch a heart of stone.

Did he relive his father's death? Or the swift, furious battle wherein he'd taken those wounds that marked his beautiful body?

While yet she contemplated it, he awoke and opened his eyes, looking every bit as disoriented as she felt. His gaze found her, and his eyes widened in shock.

"Ah, God!"

Not the way she usually found herself addressed by bonny young men, but she understood the sentiment.

He sat up and she fell back, withdrawing her reaching hand.

"Mistress MacIvor."

"Ramsay." Somehow it did not seem right to address him as "Your Highness" when he still had tears on his cheeks. Besides, Mara found it difficult to imagine the true Prince bunking on broken stone, covered with dust.

And if she could not imagine it, perhaps 'twas, as Ramsay said, an ill-fated scheme.

But nay—she could not let his attitude or her own uncertainty discourage her. She must keep her heart high. For there could be no greater honor than assisting the Prince by confounding those who would harm him.

And if she—if she and the Ramsay—did not continue with the plan, where could she go? She had no desire to return home, and had no home, for all that.

"Are you unwell?" If those wounds troubled him too badly she would need to rethink her intentions. She did not want him taking a fever and dying on her somewhere amid the heather.

He shivered in a long, slow spasm. The April air felt damp and chill, but not enough to account for such a reaction.

His expression closed; he scrambled to his feet and, without a word, went outside.

To relieve himself, no doubt—or perhaps to flee her. Mara considered it before she rose and followed him.

Aye, and she had slept far too long, slept the day away. Now evening approached, and mist lay everywhere, closed in around the round tower like a blanket. The tower had been built on a height with a commanding view, but Mara could see no farther than the length of her arm in any direction.

The Ramsay had disappeared as if he'd never existed.

She stared about anyway, with mingled anger and despair. It seemed Laird Elliot had chosen his man badly. The Ramsay had not the mettle required.

And she had failed.

The setting sun, competing with the mist, succeeded in bleeding only a dim amount of radiance. She would have to stay put until it cleared enough for her to tell her direction.

Upon the thought, something moved to her left. Ramsay came around the side of the round tower, still adjusting the front of his borrowed kilt.

Not run off, then. The air escaped Mara's lungs in a whoosh, and she spoke before thinking.

"I supposed you'd hied off."

He gave her a long, hard stare and shook his head. "Nay, mistress. Whatever I might think of this mad chase, I ha' given my word to my father and so am bound."

Honor bound. The words appeared in Mara's mind, though she did not speak them.

She merely nodded. "I wanted to get moving as soon as possible, but we will need to wait for this mist to clear. Best come inside and take something to eat."

He followed her back in, leaving tracks in the dust with his wet hose. Those would be ruined, for certain. Did he not understand how difficult it had been to come by his fine clothing?

She gave him a critical look. "The true Prince would take better care of his appearance, I am thinking."

A sour smile twitched Ramsay's lips. "Even the true Prince, if living rough, would get soiled and torn. Or," he added peevishly, "do you suppose His Great Highness does no' relieve himself like other men?"

Och, aye, the Ramsay was going to prove a

pleasure to travel beside, all the long and weary miles.

She drew her pack closer and glared into his eyes. Hoping to discomfit him, she retorted, "I do no' ken, do I? I have never spent time in the Prince's company, nor seen him naked."

"I am sure there is no' that much to tell between us." Did the Ramsay sound amused?

Mara could not imagine how even the Prince could have a finer body than his.

"Tell me, mistress, if no' the Prince, just how many men have you seen naked?"

"A few." Her brother, Robert, in passing. And Donald MacLinn when he'd taken her maidenhead— but she'd kept her eyes squeezed tight shut most of the time. And he'd kept his sark on his back, the rascal.

Ramsay smiled a real smile that put dimples in his cheeks and caused Mara's heart to skip a beat. "Aye, well then, you will be an authority." He sat down, his bad dream apparently dismissed. Did he not know she had seen those tears he shed in his sleep? She ached to ask him about his feelings but did not quite dare.

"I will warrant, though," he went on wickedly, "you would not refuse the chance to see His Highness Charlie stripped down. How close ha' you been to the man?"

"Not so close, but I did see him when he raised the clans at Glenfinnan. My da took me with him, saying he might as well persuade a pony to speak as tell me to stay home. He knew I would just ha' followed. Were you there?"

He ignored the question and instead slanted a look up at her where she stood. "I once had a pony that could speak."

Was there challenge in the statement? Did he imply he could make her obedient when her father could not? She snorted. "Did you, now? And, pray, what did he say?"

"'Twas a *she*, and she told me *Ciamar a tha thu?* every morning when I brought her breakfast. She looked a bit like you, come to think on it, with a roan mane that fell over her nose."

Mara raised a hand to her hair, still mussed from sleep. *Teasing.* The Ramsay teased her.

"Aye, well," she returned, "and now 'tis I bringing you your supper, Your Highness, so wish me 'good day' prettily."

****

They walked down off the height, through mingled mist and gloaming into clearer weather, in near silence. After their banter over supper, Mara hoped for something more. She did enjoy a natter while traveling, but Ramsay had once more shut down and assumed the mask she'd first seen on him. At least he proved no laggard and seemed prepared to cover some ground, though he refused to don the Prince's highly polished boots again and, instead, went in his stockings, now most certainly ruined.

Just before they lost the last light, Mara spied a cluster of cottages ahead. She reached out and seized Ramsay's arm, dragging him to a halt.

"This will be Munlochy, where we begin to lay our trail. You maun look the part, mind."

He returned her look stonily. "And how do we lay this trail?"

"I will go ahead, ask if the Sassenach forces have been seen since the battle, and imply I am escorting an important gentleman away to safety. You are no' to show yourself yet, do you understand?" She raked him with her gaze. "You will no' make a proper impression."

Ramsay directed his gaze at the cluster of cottages. "I do no' think it safe for you to go down there alone."

"None of this is 'safe.' I would no' have volunteered were I afraid." Volunteered? After Robert had returned injured, she had begged for the opportunity.

He snorted again, far more derisively this time. "I still say we should both go down. I may be forced to defend you with this ceremonial rapier at my side." He sneered at the sword he wore. "I am sure the 'true Prince' as you call him has never wetted his."

"You will stay here."

He ducked his head in mock obeisance. "If I don the accursed boots may I please come along, mistress?"

Dhé, the man was insufferable.

"Nay. Conceal yourself in the heather, there."

"What sort of Prince skulks in the heather? Och, aye—I see you have his measure at last."

With a huff, Mara started off down the slope to where the village appeared to drowse peacefully in the gathering gloom. She would show him how 'twas done!

Chapter Five

Diarmad paced through the fronds of young bracken while he waited for Mara MacIvor to return, far less than happy with the situation. He'd watched her walk down to the cluster of huts, the last of the light catching in her hair, and up to the door of the nearest cottage. He had seen the door open and a sliver of light spill out before she disappeared inside. Since then he had heard and seen nothing, and cursed if it felt safe to him.

Yet no one had put him in charge of Mistress MacIvor's safety. He need not assume responsibility for her. Indeed, were she captured or killed, would that not negate the promise he had made to his father? For he could scarcely go on laying a false trail by himself when he did not know the chosen route.

Still, he did not wish for harm to befall Mistress MacIvor—'twould be a damned shame, that. She had a certain mad courage and enough fire to snare the interest of any man, even if she had tossed away her sense and misplaced her loyalty.

In love with Charles Edward she must be—or at least smitten, as women tended to become. He wondered with sudden, sharp curiosity just how far her services might extend were she guiding the true Prince and not just Diarmad Ramsay, a poor imitation. She had made no secret of the fact that she thought Diarmad just that. Traveling alone with the Stuart, would she extend every comfort? Lie down in the fronds of new bracken and welcome him with that lovely body of hers? How warm and sweet would she be when he plunged inside?

To his surprise, he found himself stirring beneath his kilt while contemplating the question. Given the grief he carried, how could he even consider such a thing?

Upon the thought, he heard a sudden cry from below—something between a scream and a shout. He spun where he stood. So distracted had he been by the idea of Mistress MacIvor spreading her legs for him, he had lost track of the passing time; now the dark had deepened all around.

Emotions flooded through him, the same he believed he'd left back on the battlefield or at his father's death bed: protest and desperate protectiveness.

What harm had befallen her?

No sooner did that question blossom in his mind than he saw Mara burst from the door of the cottage below; a man clad in a Sassenach's uniform followed, snagged her arm, and hauled her back inside.

Diarmad, reacting without thought, sprang forward, speared by the rage that rose to his head. He charged down the slope on his stockinged feet, the Prince's poor excuse for a sword already in his hand, a cry stuck in his throat. He had entrusted his own sword to Elliot, to be returned to him when this mad duty was done. He had only the thin rapier and his long knife with which he'd refused to part.

He heard raised voices as he pelted down into the tiny village, which to the eye appeared mostly deserted. Aye, and that alone should have made them suspicious.

Patrols of Sassenach soldiers now roamed the hills all around; had they already cleared out this village?

No one but a collie saw him as he gained the road and continued running. He virtually skidded to a halt at the door of the cottage, now open, and looked inside.

The light from within fair blinded him after the soft twilight, but he espied what appeared to be far too many people for the given space. A woman—not Mara but far shorter—cradled two children to her bosom over against one wall, facing a number of soldiers. Blinking and peering further, he saw Mara, captive, struggling in the arms of a Sassenach.

With a roar, rapier raised, he catapulted in. A number of surprised faces, including Mara's, turned toward him. Diarmad counted five soldiers, all heavily armed.

The first to speak, Mara cried, "Your Highness!"

Damn her, Diarmad thought, even as the first soldier exclaimed in reaction and turned to face him. Instinct took over then—the same Cainnech had drilled into him on so many bright mornings when Diarmad would have much rather been off running the hills.

Cainnech.

The narrow, half-blunted point of the rapier took the first soldier in the throat, and the man fell like a sack of rocks amidst a bright shower of blood.

"Leave go of her," he snarled to the next man, and when the fellow responded by shoving Mara at his companions and drawing his sword, they engaged one another.

Sassenach weapons might be vastly inferior to a Highland claymore, but as Diarmad knew, not many of the Highlanders fighting at Culloden had possessed claymores. His own sword, while of good quality and much better than this piece of shite with which he now found himself armed, had been just a sword.

Yet somehow he made his current weapon serve. He opened his opponent's left shoulder and then got in under the man's guard and pierced his heart. The soldier fell with a thud.

Three men left. Two immediately came at him, leaving Mara in the grip of the last. Diarmad heard one of them utter the name "Charles Edward" even as he drew his long knife from his belt.

The next moments proved fast and furious. The man on the left got in a slash that opened Diarmad's forearm. He paid for it with a wound to the neck and went down.

Diarmad, his eyes now fully adapted to the light, measured his fourth opponent, who stood in front of Mara and her captor. The fellow had an ugly, sneering face and held his sword competently, as if he knew how to use it.

Before the brute could move, Diarmad leaped and planted a kick to his gut with both feet. The fellow tumbled back into Mara and her captor, and before he could recover Diarmad fell on him. The scent of blood welled in a hot rush as Diarmad cut his throat.

"Well, now." He drew himself up and regarded the last of the Sassenach soldiers, who looked a bit green, with the same controlled rage that had possessed him back on the battlefield. "You will leave go of her."

The man shook his head. He had his knife up at Mara's throat but, to give the lass credit, she did not appear so terrified as she should.

"Aye, so," Diarmad sneered at the soldier, "you

maun wish to die."

The fellow responded by pressing his blade against Mara's milk-white neck; a thin line of red appeared there.

The rapier moved, so swiftly even Diarmad could not track it, and embedded itself in the soldier's right shoulder. Fingers suddenly unresponsive, the man dropped his knife and gasped.

One gasp, two, before the blade ended his life.

All at once they stood in the midst of carnage—he and Mara staring at one another, and the woman standing frozen behind.

A child wailed, snagging Diarmad's attention. The woman had their faces pressed to her breasts.

Before he could regret what they had just witnessed, their mother breathed, "Your Highness!" and sank into a rough curtsy.

"Och, nay," he cried hoarsely. "Get up."

"Your Highness," Mara echoed and sank down also, her eyes fixed to his, bright and beseeching. The wench thought to use this as an opportunity to lay her false trail, did she? With five men dead.

"I am meant to guide and defend you, Your Highness," she said. "Not the other way 'round!"

Diarmad became aware of other people at his back, filling the doorway. He spun with the rapier at the ready but saw no uniforms, only villagers—neighbors, no doubt, come to gaze on the spectacle.

"Get up, mistress," he told the woman again. "Comfort your children."

She arose, but only in order to clasp Diarmad's hand, which she pressed to her lips. "Thank you, Your Highness, for delivering us from those monsters! They would have had their way with the young woman and me also. You see, my husband has no' yet come back from the battle."

And likely would not, Diarmad thought soberly. What would become of this little family?

"They were looking for our men what fled the fighting," said an old woman from the doorway. "They would have been happy to seize you, Your Highness! *Dhé*, and I never knew Your Highness for so great a swordsman."

"Nor did I." Mara got to her feet, still gazing at Diarmad like a woman in a dream.

"Brave lass," said the old woman, "to guide our Prince away to safety. Come ye wi' me, and I will show you the best route to take."

Diarmad, the breath still rushing in his lungs, gestured at the fallen men with his rapier. "But—"

"We shall clear away that mess," assured another woman, from the doorway, "and burn it all. Ye go wi' Annie now, Your Blessed Highness."

"Wait."

Diarmad bent down and rifled through the pockets of the first man who'd challenged him and who he now saw wore the insignia of a captain. "He may have orders that will prove useful to us."

Diarmad found no orders but did come up with a heavy leather purse, the contents of which he shared out among the villagers.

"Keep that," he said as he pressed most of it into his hostess's hands, "in case your husband does not return."

Again she sank to her knees and pressed her face against his hand. "If I ha' lost him in the service of such a Prince as yoursel', I can but count it an honor, Your Highness!"

Thoroughly shaken, Diarmad nevertheless lifted the captain's sword and boots before following the old woman—Annie—from the cottage with Mara at his back. He listened carefully while the woman described a route that should take them safely north and westward.

Annie concluded by laying a finger to her lips. "And nary a word shall pass about ye having been here, Your Highness." Her bleary eyes filled with tears. "And 'tis the honor of my life to ha' met ye!"

Diarmad clasped the old woman's bony hand. "Nay, 'tis I who stand honored by the loyalty of those such as yoursel'. I admire your courage."

Annie bowed her head and stood like a woman who had received a benediction while Mara gathered her pack and other burdens from the cottage, and they walked off.

Neither of them spoke for many moments as they left the dwellings and climbed back toward the heights in the gathering gloom.

Then Mara shot Diarmad an intense look. "Well, I must say you left an impression back there. No doubt they will keep a fond remembrance of their Prince."

Diarmad smiled grimly.

"And the largesse made a noble touch," she mused on.

"That first woman's husband is no' likely to return. What will she do, with two weans to raise?"

Mara shrugged. "What will any of us do? She would fare far better beneath the rule of the true Prince's father than that poor excuse for a king who now holds the throne."

"You think so?" Diarmad did not feel so certain. What might Charles Edward, who had saved himself at Culloden, do for such humble folk?

Mara shot him another look. "I had no idea you were such a braw fighter."

Braw, was it? Suddenly Diarmad felt utterly weary. Five more souls—granted, Sassenach souls—added to the harvest he had already taken.

Aye, and did he care that he might strike Mara MacIvor favorably with his prowess? He eyed her with speculation. Perhaps. For that image he'd had of her while up on the hillside still lingered in his mind.

"By any road," she mused on, "you could no' have done better with planting the notion the Prince has come this way."

"They promised not to tell."

"And they will no'. They are loyal subjects of their true king, even more so now. Yet such news tends to travel if only in whispers."

Diarmad grunted. All he'd done was add to the legend of the man he despised so deeply.

He threw himself down in the shelter of a boulder and began stripping the hose from his feet. Mara, forced to pause also, planted her fists on her hips. "What are you doing?"

"These are ruined, and I think the Sassenach's boots will fit better than the Prince's."

"You canno' go about wearing the boots of a Sassenach—nor carrying his sword."

"Why not? Think of them as trophies of battle."

"Charles Edward would no' sink to such a lowly deed."

Diarmad shot her a burning look. "And has Charles Edward ever preserved your virtue?"

All the indignation drained from Mara's tense form. "Nay, and I should thank you."

"Aye, you should."

"They would have raped me, and that woman—in front of her bairns."

"Aye, but"—he paused with a boot in his hand—"I do not doubt you would ha' considered it a worthy sacrifice made for His Highness."

"Do not be daft." To his surprise she sat down beside him. "Are you badly hurt? I saw you take that stroke to your arm. We had best wrap it up before we move on."

She drew her pack toward her but did not root around in it. Instead, her gaze fixed to Diarmad's, she said, "I am thankful, Ramsay. I would not wish to endure such a fate."

When he did not reply, she continued, "I ha' only ever been with one man. So while you may not ha' precisely spared my virtue, which was in truth lost to him, you have spared me much pain and shame."

Diarmad stared at her. He wondered who the man was she'd blessed with her favor. Did they have an understanding? Did she love and long to return to him?

He scolded, "'Twas gey foolish for you to go walking into such a trap. It canno' happen again."

She leaned closer, and for one mad moment Diarmad thought she meant to kiss him. But she only whispered the words, strangely seductive in the bright air, "Aye, Your Highness."

Chapter Six

Mara shifted position on the stony ground and wondered for the hundredth time why she could not sleep. They had trudged throughout the night and on into the next day, ducking like harts or hares over brae and through glen, laying what she no longer doubted must be a dangerous trail. By noontime, strain and reaction to what had happened earlier rendered her weary enough to fall down, and she found a place deep in a copse of rowan trees where they might lie over till dark found them again.

Diarmad—"His Highness"—had ceased complaint and become strangely biddable, walking in his stolen boots. Under the trees, he soon settled beneath his ragged plaid to sleep.

Now Mara, giving it up as a bad bet, sat up and went to peer out from beneath the newly leafed branches. The gloaming, which came early at this time of year, once more grayed the scenery, and she strained to focus. She could not chase the scene from the cottage out of her mind; it left her strangely breathless thinking again on the way the Ramsay had flown to her rescue. Never had she seen a man fight so—not even her brother. Diarmad had been all flying hair and bright steel, fierce as a north wind. Even the poor quality of the weapon in his hand had not hampered him.

Mara shivered where she crouched, not an arm's

reach away from Ramsay. He still slept quietly; no evil dreams for him this time.

Mara scrutinized the countryside again, wracked by her thoughts. An honest woman, she had to admit she may have gone into this venture without sufficient consideration. It might well prove far more dangerous than she had estimated when first she heard it described. Then her heart had risen to the glory of undertaking such a task on the Prince's behalf—being near him in deed if not flesh—and her loyalty bade her make any sacrifice.

Aye, well, her loyalty held true. She feared little on her own behalf, though she had never been so glad to see anyone as when the Ramsay flew through the door and kept her from being forced by five Sassenachs. For she had no doubt things would have ended so, had he not intervened.

And, she asked herself sternly, would that have been too much to sacrifice on behalf of her Prince? She stared into the lowering darkness above her head, not even a star shining, and struggled to decide. She supposed she could survive the ordeal—women did. But she suspected if such a horror befell her she would never be quite the same.

Her sole experience with Donald MacLinn following the midsummer festival last year had proved surprisingly quick and fumbling, not wholly enjoyable on her part. But she had been curious about the great mystery of coupling, and willing.

Now her native honesty bade her admit a truth that shocked her. Were she to lie with anyone again, she would choose Diarmad Ramsay.

Was that what made her so restless now? Thinking

about his strong, supple body and the way he had turned it into a lethal weapon last evening? The dangerous grace with which he had moved, the shoddy rapier flashing, not a wasted motion as he took the Sassenachs down one by one?

Just remembering it enflamed her. She wondered what it would be like if those quick, strong hands of his touched her, if she lay beneath him while he poured himself into her—and she ached so badly for it she could not lie still.

'Twould be nothing like Donald's clumsy ministrations. But her relationship with Diarmad Ramsay was awkward, at best; surely she would never find out.

"Mara?" His voice came out of the trees and made her start. "Is someone there?"

"Nay, but we should be off and moving soon." And had the wicked thoughts in her mind somehow waked him?

"You got little enough rest. What is the matter?"

Mara smiled ruefully. What if she told him, as honesty bade? What would the gallant Ramsay do then? Might he supply that for which she longed, before they moved off down the brae? Just the thought made her heart begin to pound.

But before she could speak he suggested, "I suppose the madness of what you—we—are about has finally struck you."

"Madness?" Mara repeated.

"Folly, or whatever you wish to call it."

"I am only thinking of what would have happened had you no' followed me down off the hill—against my bidding, I might add. I must thank you."

"You already have, or did you forget?"

Aye, but Mara did not mean to thank him with words. Shocked at herself all over again, she remained silent.

"Try to sleep," he bade. "As soon as it is full dark, you will need all your wits and strength to lay your bonny Prince's false trail."

"You hate him." Mara clearly heard the loathing in Ramsay's voice. "And him your rightful Prince!"

"I do no' hate him so much as what he has done. I saw it, Mistress MacIvor, how men died while he spared himself."

"As he must! He is the Cause, and without him there is no future."

"There is no future for some of us now."

"Why did you agree to do this, if your heart is turned so fierce against him?" She answered herself before he could. "Aye, so—you promised your father."

Ramsay had no chance to correct her. Above their heads the sky abruptly opened and rain began to hiss down.

Mara, a true daughter of the Highlands, had been bred to ignore the weather, and rain in particular. She did not so much mind walking in it or performing her chores back home, but she knew this signaled the end to any remaining chance of sleep, and she exclaimed in dismay.

Ramsay snorted and moved impatiently. "Are you cold? Come here, then."

"Eh?" Mara scarcely believed her ears.

"I am lying dry under an overhang. You take my place."

"We will share it." Mara decided and moved before

41

she could think better of it or he could object. "And you can warm me while we wait for the rain to ease."

She scrambled over the rocky ground and dove into the depths of the copse where he lay. His body stiffened as she eased in beside him, but that did not dissuade her. The rain no longer touched her here and, aye, it did feel warmer.

Ramsay drew a breath even as the heat of his body wrapped around her. She could now catch the scent particular to him—spicy, fresh, and rampantly male, with the tang of Highland air caught in his hair and clothing. Would he push her away?

He sounded amused when he spoke, his voice vibrating deep in her ear. "I suppose this must satisfy some wish you have of lying with your Prince."

It satisfied a wish, right enough, but had nothing to do with Charles Edward. Mara retorted, "My only intention is to lie out of the wet and grow warm. Will you complain about us sharing against the chill?"

"And about having my arms full of bonny lass? Nay."

He thought her bonny. Or did he just tease as he had before? Mara ached to know, and desire rose to her head like a draught of her Da's whisky.

She slewed round in her allotted space until she faced him, her mouth just below his. "I am no' thinking of the Prince," she confessed, "but still how I might thank you properly for your braw gallantry."

"Och, aye?" Did he sound as breathless as she? "And what to your mind would make a proper thank-you?"

Without further words, she pressed her mouth to his. His lips felt warm and surprisingly soft, and their touch sent a spear of need through Mara, blazing in its intensity. Surely she had been born for this, for him.

He made a sound deep in his throat—protest or enjoyment? She could not tell. Again she expected him to push her away; instead his hand came up and cradled her cheek. His lips molded to hers, coaxed and persuaded them apart.

Mara, not in the habit of feeling helpless, found she had no strength to resist. She opened to him readily and his tongue plunged into her mouth in an act of reckless possession.

And oh, she could taste him—his essence, wild and sweet, flowed upon her senses and heat coursed through her body even as her heart took up a powerful, shuddering rhythm.

She could no longer breathe. She no longer wanted to. She would gladly starve for air if it meant she could stay here in his arms.

Slowly and surely his tongue explored the inside of her mouth and her blood caught fire. Even when Donald had entered her—the act brief, hasty, and indeed not without discomfort—Mara had never known such intimacy. She opened all of herself to the Ramsay in complete, if silent, offering and could have wept when he broke the kiss and withdrew his lips from hers.

"Now," he whispered, "that is what I call a proper thank-you."

And Mara shocked herself all over again by returning, "Not enough, by half."

She pressed her mouth to his once more, open and inviting. Not loathe to take advantage, he deepened the kiss and set up a tingle low in Mara's abdomen.

His fingers, splayed against her cheek, moved into

her hair, where they tangled among the wild curls. He steadied her while his tongue found the back of hers and began to thrust in a tantalizing dance. Mara's bones promptly turned to water, and she knew she would, at this moment, give him anything.

Anything.

She caressed the delightful strength of his tongue with her own and the taste of him filled her. Who knew a man could claim a woman this way, imprint himself upon her, make her doubt she could continue to live without him?

He made another sound, satisfaction this time, as she stroked his tongue with hers. He shifted his weight, sliding over her, and she instinctively parted her thighs. Her hands burrowed beneath his plaid, inside the fine sark, and found warm flesh.

Aye, and she had wanted this ever since she saw him standing naked, since she tended his wounds. She slid her palms over supple muscle sprinkled with hair and came alive with delight. She might touch him so forever and not have enough.

He broke the kiss again and his breath came ragged. "Just how far does this gratitude of yours extend, Mistress MacIvor?"

"I do no' ken, do I?" Honest as ever, Mara admitted the truth. Caught in this moment, would she make a gift of herself to him? Could she imagine doing anything else? "I ha' not thought so far ahead."

"You make it difficult to think at all." He buried his warm mouth in her neck and her delight blossomed unbearably. She felt his lips on her flesh and then—by heaven, was that his tongue?

Easy, far too easy to surrender to the lure of

sensation. But if she did, what would happen when this magical time they spent together ended and the real world came sweeping back in?

Chapter Seven

A dream—aye, surely so it must be. For Mistress Mara MacIvor could not in truth lie in Diarmad's arms, warm, sweet and willing. All men had such dreams from time to time, and he knew he had been asleep only moments ago. He knew also that, awake, he and Mistress MacIvor did not get on well enough to afford these kinds of liberties.

And, aye, no woman had ever tasted so good, save in his dreams. Still and all, could a mere dream seem so real? For he could hear the cold rain pattering down out beyond the overhang; he could feel Mara's breath soft on his cheek. He felt the silk of her hair between his fingers and caught the beguiling scent of her, which aroused him all out of proportion.

But did he not remember waking to hear her, restless? Had she not fled from the rain and squeezed in with him? *Dhé*, perhaps it was real after all.

He itched to test the genuineness of it. In truth, he desired far more, wanted to hike up the skirt that covered her legs and plunge into her over and over again. But she did not even favor him. What if she cried rape, a fate from which he had only just saved her?

Yet his blood ran hot as fire, and she tasted so damn good on his tongue.

He drew his hand from her hair and reached for the laces on her bodice—a test of his dream, for surely she would stop him if he dared too much.

Her breath hitched as his fingers tugged at the string, but she did not object. He felt her heartbeat shake her breast beneath his hand.

Her breast. He succeeded with the lace, and her bodice fell open; he slid his hand inside.

Warm, warm, soft, and sheer heaven to touch. Her breast, the perfect size, lay ripe in his hand, making his mouth go dry. He longed to taste.

With his thumb, he found her nipple, a tight bud in the mound of softness, and she moaned like a woman in pain. Aye, now, if ever, she would object and push him away.

"Please," she gasped. With her own hand she pulled at her bodice so it opened farther, and arched her back, offering herself to him.

Heat rose to Diarmad's head even before he bent to take her breast. He tasted her first with his tongue, a dance that took him all around her nipple, before he latched on and suckled deep.

"Ah, God!" The words came from her like prayer. She caught his head between her hands, but only to urge him closer, a silent appeal for more.

Aye, and he wanted to taste her everywhere, longed to work his way down her body from her delicate breasts to where she kept her well of heat. He also wanted to thrust himself into her hot mouth, though he doubted he would make three thrusts before exploding like a green lad.

Yet a few shreds of sanity remained. Aye, she seemed warm and willing now, but what about when this heat abated? He'd been entrusted with her care, not given leave to use her for his pleasure.

Summoning strength from somewhere, he released her breast and raised his head. He could not see her face clearly in the gloom beneath the overhang, but thought she had her eyes squeezed shut.

Did she not wish to see him? Sudden doubt came rushing. Did she imagine she lay beneath the true Prince, offering him the ultimate comfort?

Maybe she did not want him, Diarmad Ramsay, at all.

"Please," she beseeched again, "do no' stop."

He did not want to stop. Neither would he play the imposter to her fantasy.

Very softly, he mused, "Do you ken what you are asking?"

"Aye." Her breath still came quick, and he could feel every beat of her heart. Deliberately, he slid his hand down her leg and raised her skirt, trailing his fingers as he went.

She quickened beneath him and parted her legs still further.

"You are no' a maiden?" he confirmed.

"Nay." Wildly, she reached for his mouth and kissed him again. He took advantage and slid his hand all the way up.

He wondered again with whom she had lain. Some buck of Clan MacIvor who had then gone off and tossed his life away in her beloved Cause? At least he, Diarmad, need not worry about doing damage to her maidenhead.

And, God bless her, she wore nothing at all beneath her skirt and chemise. His fingers encountered only heat and a cluster of damp curls. She moaned into his mouth demandingly.

'Twould be the easiest thing to slide into her. But if this were no mad dream, she might well hate him for it later. Women were capricious that way.

She lifted her hips to meet his hand. With his tongue deep in her mouth he thrust one finger inside her, and a second.

Holy heaven, she was ready for him, tight and slick. He would be mad not to take advantage.

Aye so, then, he must be mad.

He broke the kiss one more time, drew his fingers from her with a heroic feat of will, and brushed her skirt back down.

"Mistress MacIvor, nay."

"What? Why?"

"You neither like nor favor me. And I feel I am charged wi' protecting you, not—"

She said nothing but clung to him with her hands, and one ankle curled about his leg.

Hastily, he disentangled his limbs and arose, nearly braining himself on the overhang. Beneath the Prince's vile kilt, he stood hard as iron.

"We ha' a duty to accomplish together," he told her stiffly. "This—'twill just complicate matters."

"Will it?"

"Without question."

A lengthy silence fell, during which Diarmad heard her struggle to master her breathing. He wondered if her bodice still lay open and wished he could see.

"But," she said at last, wicked and daring, "I ha' not finished with thanking you."

Diarmad reeled where he stood. Almost, he dropped back down upon her, almost accepted what she offered and to hell with the regret.

Instead, he shook his head and stepped out into the rain.

****

Diarmad Ramsay must not find her pleasing. Mara, lying there in the gloom, fixed on that as the only explanation for his abandonment of her. Most young men of her acquaintance seemed to spend half their time and energy seeking what she had just offered the Ramsay. She did not think many would refuse.

So for all his talk of duty, he must think her ugly—perhaps wild, or overly bold. Perhaps he liked his women chaste and unassuming.

That could never describe Mara MacIvor.

Yet he had kissed her as if he wanted her. Touched her that way, as well. And she had felt him hard and ready beneath his borrowed kilt.

She must repel him in some way so that, even despite his arousal, he turned from her.

Ah, but what was she to do now that she had tasted him, had that flavor on her tongue? How keep from wanting to touch him now she knew how it felt? Because, just like that, she needed him, fiercely, as she needed air.

Beautiful, maddening, heroic devil of a man.

She raised both hands and pressed them to her mouth. How would she ever face him when they set out walking together? Given he came back out of the rain and had not walked off, never to return.

Aye, and if she had chased him off with her unseemly passion, what did that mean to the carefully laid plan? She would disappoint her father and all the others who sought to assure the Prince's safety, perhaps even endanger Charlie.

Worse, she might never see Diarmad Ramsay again.

The pain of that thought urged her up, shivering. She scrambled to her feet, tied her bodice hastily, and stepped out into the onrushing night.

"Ramsay!"

No reply. The gray, wet evening seemed to press in all around her. She could still hear the rain falling in a steady rhythm, but not so much as a footfall.

"Diarmad!"

"Whisht, lass!" He appeared suddenly out of the gloom beside her. "Why do you no' just holler out our location?"

Mara huffed. "I thought you had gone."

"I merely sought to cool my blood."

He admitted it then, that she had aroused him. Wild hope leaped in her heart.

She said, "I know a better cure than the cold rain."

"Aye, so you do. But damned if I will take advantage of it."

She ached to ask him why. There in the shadowed gloaming, with the veil of wet falling all around, she wondered what kept the words from her lips. Usually she did not lack in the courage to say aught that came into her head, but now, perhaps, she did not truly wish to know.

Because if this man, even now standing so close she could feel his heat, intended never to complete what had been started back there, if Mara were left with this unfulfilled ache, she did not know that she could handle the frustration.

No sooner had the thought expressed itself in her mind than he reached out and touched her shoulder lightly.

"Go back where 'tis dry and try to rest," he bade.

Rest? He expected her to lie still—perhaps sleep—while her body still vibrated from being so near him?

"But that is your bed."

"It canno' be long till these clouds move off and the rain lessens. I will stay on watch."

"You think a troop of the King's men will be out in this wet?"

"I'll take no chances." A rueful edge colored his voice when he went on, "And the rain may help me guard against temptation."

Mara scowled, the annoyance he roused so easily in her rising. Yet even then she longed to move into his arms, ached to persuade him with her lips, convince him to accompany her back inside. Instead, with a meekness her father and brother would never recognize, she returned to the copse.

He had taken his plaid with him against the wet, but the place where he'd been lying still smelled faintly of him. Mara cuddled in tight and spent the interval until the rain lessened questioning her own sanity.

Chapter Eight

The persistent rain accompanied them for two days and nights while they slogged over soaking hillsides—cold, spring rain that made the journey miserable and difficult. With their supply of food all but gone, Mara began spending the coin Laird Elliot had given her for just that purpose, stopping by dwellings in the smallest villages on her own while Ramsay waited on the hillside. To the householders with whom she bargained she always alluded to pursuing a most secret mission, hinted that she guided a personage vital to the future of the Highlands.

By the widening of their eyes and the parting of their lips, she could tell they took her meaning. She believed most of them loyal to the bone, yet one old man living alone in a shieling, so weak he could barely stand, asked her if she had heard of the great price the Crown had set on Prince Charles Edward's head.

"Not that anyone would betray the bonny lad," the man had added, his gaze fervent. Yet the hair stood up on the back of Mara's neck, and she had to remind herself this was the very reason they had set out on their journey—to court pursuit and take the heat from the true Prince.

She also told herself she must now be doubly on guard against being tracked and captured. For surely news of their passing must reach the wrong—or was it the right?—ears soon enough. So far they had caught no glimpse of any Crown troops, save once at a distance when they passed the large town of Dingwall, giving it a wide berth.

They spoke little, and not at all of what had happened back in the rowan copse. Mara did not even have the heart to chastise Ramsay for wearing his own plaid—identifying as a beacon— since it kept off the wet. But those moments spent in his arms remained constantly bright in her mind and, she suspected, Diarmad's. For he avoided looking her full in the eyes, and when they bedded down he made sure to lie as far from her as he could arrange.

And so Mara went over the hills cold, wet, and frustrated. She still wanted Diarmad Ramsay so much she ached with it. Now her natural tendency to express her worry and fill the time with chatter had once more been stunted.

While she should have been concentrating on the dangers all around them and on staying ahead of pursuers, her thoughts instead danced in her mind, contemplating things she wanted to ask him but did not dare. Had he a woman waiting for him in his home glen in the far north, someone to whom he was promised? Might that explain his rejection of her, Mara?

For it still stung. She might not be beautiful like her older sister, Flora, long married and gone from the family home. But men of her acquaintance tended to find her worth the chasing. Many had looked after her with interest.

She had bared her breasts for few.

Upon that thought she now turned and shot a look at the man who followed her through the wet without complaint. His soaking plaid lay about his face, nearly obscuring those eyes that seemed to see right through her—or would, if he actually looked at her. Several days' growth of beard gathered about those fine lips of his, making Mara long to touch.

She did love a man with a beard.

"Hie," he whispered suddenly. "Someone is coming."

So there was. Mara's heart leaped sickeningly. On point and supposedly guiding him, she should have seen them first—or at least heard them. But she had allowed herself to become perilously distracted.

Ramsay caught her arm, pulling her off the faint trail they had been following and down into the young bracken.

She could hear them clearly then—almost on top of her and Ramsay, coming out of the mist and rain. Horses, the jingle of harness, a gruff word or two. A small troop of English guard hove into view, and Mara stopped breathing.

Do not let them look aside. For she and Ramsay lay only poorly hidden. Even upon the thought she felt his arm, draped protectively over her shoulders, press her down. At the same moment he eased his stolen sword from its scabbard.

One, two, three, four—she lost count of the company, but they made more than eight, all mounted—clearly a detail out combing the hills for someone.

For the lass of whom they had heard, guiding a man who just might be Charles Edward.

Abruptly the captain riding at their head held up a hand. The company halted just past the place where

Mara and Ramsay lay.

"Did you hear something?" the captain demanded of his men.

Surely his ears could not have caught the whisper of Ramsay's sword being drawn. The sound of the falling rain must obscure nearly everything.

Mara squinted at the man, squat on his horse and about forty years of age. Possibly he followed an instinct, as Da said the best warriors did—even Sassenach warriors.

None of his men immediately responded. They looked thoroughly wet and far from eager to chase any quarry through the bracken.

At last the man who rode behind the captain—his second in command?—ventured, "Deer, sir? I see some over there."

The company all looked away to the west. Ramsay took the opportunity to shove Mara's bright head farther down.

"Yes, no doubt," the captain decided. "We will ride on to the nearest town and see can we find a dry place to spend the night."

They moved off with a clatter, but the pressure of Ramsay's arm kept Mara flat in the bracken long after, until she began to squirm.

"Let me up. They are gone."

"I am no' so certain. That captain looks to have a sharp eye and a sharper mind. They may just double back."

Mara subsided, taking advantage of his nearness to lean into him. His hair brushed her cheek, and she caught the beguiling scent of him even above that of peaty soil and damp vegetation. Her body began to tingle in response.

Warm he felt, amid the wet. An irresistible haven.

She strained her ears, listening. Distraction with the fine Ramsay had nearly cost them dear. She could not allow that to happen again.

"I am that sorry," she whispered when it became plain the troop would not return. "I was on point and should have heard them."

He made no reply but gazed at her from mere inches away. Even in the gloom of the day his eyes shone clear and blue-gray.

What did he see when he looked at her? A poor excuse for a guardian? A foolish lass? A wanton? Cursed if Mara cared. She wanted to press her lips to his so badly it hurt.

"You no longer look much like the Prince." She waved a hand. "Not with that beard."

He grimaced and rubbed his jaw with long, brown fingers. *Those fingers had been inside her*. For an instant, the memory turned Mara faint.

"Do no' say you are going to make me shave. Surely even your sacred Prince would let his beard grow out here."

"Perhaps." Unable to resist, she gazed at his pleasing features. "Tell me something, Ramsay: have you a betrothed at home?"

He hesitated. Still gazing into the depths of his eyes, she saw a shadow pass. "Nay."

"Ah. Is there someone perhaps not promised, yet dear to your heart?"

He turned his head and stared away, which benefitted Mara little since she found his profile equally pleasing.

"There is a lass."

Mara's heart sank like a rock.

"But she is betrothed to another."

"I see. A pledge of convenience, or one of the heart?"

His lips twisted in a rueful smile. "You ken, I could never tell. A woman of duty, Una keeps her true feelings close to her breast."

Una, eh? The lovely Una, no doubt a woman of grace and pleasing propriety, sharing absolutely no characteristics with wild Mara MacIvor. Well, whoever she might be, how could she fail to love and desire this man?

"Aye," she said through a suddenly tight throat, "and to whom is she betrothed?"

That made him shoot her a rueful glance. "My brother, Cainnech, no less—he who is now Chief in my father's stead."

"But I thought—that is, Master Elliot said your brother did not survive the battle. 'Tis why you took his place, is it not?"

"He did no' come away with the rest of us. That does no' mean he did no' survive. He could lie injured somewhere—he might have been taken prisoner. I think if he were dead, I would know."

"Are the two of you very close?"

"Aye. He has always been a hero to me, and the perfect older brother. As long as I can remember I ha' looked up to him."

And so would never think to charm away the woman destined for him. But if Cainnech had fallen, the place of Chief would come to Diarmad. And Una with it?

Mara squirmed uneasily in the wet bracken.

Diarmad jerked his head toward where the troop had disappeared. "They will get word of our passing soon enough and, perhaps, come after us."

"Those who ha' seen us may be too loyal to speak."

"But is that no' the point of this mad undertaking? As I asked you before, what good the hare if the hounds do not glimpse him?"

"Aye," Mara admitted unhappily. Endangering him had seemed a different prospect before she met him, touched him.

Kissed him.

"Either way," he told her unequivocally, "we had better move on."

****

The rain ended soon after dark, and a magnificent sky opened up, cleared by a chilly wind. A reef of stars emerged overhead, and Mara paused at last by the shore of a lochan.

Just where were they? Somewhere north of Dingwall and west of Tain, as alone in this wild place as two people could be.

Mara shivered where she stood; two days spent drenched to the skin and now a chilly wind. It would be a cold night.

"Do you mean to layover here?" Ramsay had taken pity on her halfway through the day and shouldered one of the packs. He set it down now, and she gave him a searching look.

"Are you very weary?" she returned. He had not complained about the long hours trudging and seemed as if he could walk forever in his stolen boots. Twice had Mara doubled back in an effort to see if they were being followed, but the hounds had apparently not taken their scent.

Now she wrapped her arms about herself and wondered for the first time if, as the Ramsay repeatedly said, this venture might be doomed. What did she accomplish out here with him? What, besides stoking the fire of her desire with his nearness.

Suddenly the world seemed an unimaginably dreary place—death behind them and perhaps ahead. What would become of her?

"I am willing to rest or go on," he told her. "No matter. But you are cold."

"I wish we might have a fire. I dare not."

His arm came around her shoulder, and he drew her close against his side. Damp and as chilled as she, he nevertheless felt marvelously warm, a comforting presence.

"Come, I will build you a nest."

He led her a few steps to a cluster of pines. There she stood very like a lost child while he pulled bracken and piled it to make a bed beneath the boughs.

"There now," he told her. "You burrow in. I will find some food in the pack and take first watch."

Wordlessly, Mara obeyed. The young bracken fronds cut the wind, and when she burrowed inside as instructed, Ramsay spread his plaid over all.

Aye, and a good thing he had kept the half-ruined thing after all.

"We are running low on food again," he observed in a low voice, knowing as well as she how sound carried on a clear night. Mara could hear the waves lapping at the edge of the lochan, and she was all too aware of Ramsay's every movement. When he at last came crawling into the nest, her senses reared to attention.

"Here." He placed a chunk of stale bannock in her hand. "Eat that. You will soon be warm."

"Aye." She felt better already with his body so close. "Where did you learn this trick for making a shelter?"

"Out hunting with Cainnech, back in the days when I ne'er dreamed my life could come apart at the seams. Tell me, Mistress MacIvor, have you been begging this food from the holdings we pass?"

"Nay, Laird Elliot gave me coin with which to buy provisions. The Prince would have a surfeit of coin, would he not?" All at once the welfare of Charles Edward did not seem so immediate and vital. Not when Mara could feel Ramsay's shoulder pressed to hers and the length of him all down her side.

He grunted. "I wonder if these Sassenachs have put a price on his head."

"They have," she admitted reluctantly, remembering the words of the old man with whom she'd bargained for provisions. The oldster had not actually named that price. It could be as little as five pounds, yet seem a king's—or a Prince's— ransom to him. "A right high one, I expect. But 'twill not matter, for no one will betray him, whatever the price."

"You think not? Do you ken how many men died in yon battle, back there? Their bairns and widows will be starving—as if they were not beforehand."

"Still, their hearts will remain true," Mara insisted.

"We shall see. Finish your supper and get some sleep. 'Tis what you need, lass. I will keep watch."

Was that kindness Mara heard in Ramsay's voice? Obediently, she hunkered down and closed her eyes, her weary body easing for the first time in days.

She would worry about the morrow when it came.

Chapter Nine

A persistent sound teased Diarmad's ear, penetrating the deep layers of his sleep. He opened his eyes and struggled for memory. He had kept first watch last evening beneath the ice-cold stars while Mara burrowed into the shelter he'd made and at last stopped her shivering. At some point during the night she had appeared at his side and bidden him go take her place. The last he knew, she was stationed, on guard, just outside the mouth of the shelter where he lay.

Now darkness still hovered beyond the pine boughs, and the susurration of waves from the lochan came to him discordantly. Aye, he heard the sound of the water—and something else besides. Where was Mara? He sat up, and the bracken bed rustled. He saw her then, no more than a dark shadow huddled in the open doorway. She waved a frantic arm in his direction, a clear demand for silence.

Alarm and relief tangled together inside him. She was all right, but surely that was a voice speaking at a near distance. Nay, a number of them.

He strained his ears and caught intelligible words. "They came this way, I tell you, and must be nearby. My nose is never wrong." Deep and gravelly, the tone lifted the hairs on Diarmad's arms.

"Your nose," another male voice jeered.

"Aye, Marcus, and ha' you ever known it to be

mistaken? We owe our fortune to this nose, so we do."

Soldiers? But nay, these were Scottish voices—and Highland. Refugees from the battle? Perhaps so. Dangerous?

Och, aye. Every instinct told him so, and he gathered himself, preparing to move despite Mara's wave to caution. He felt for his sword and found it within reach on the ground. And his long knife? There, also.

His ear caught a laugh. "Better if your nose led us to a woman."

"One of them is a woman, I tell you. So those villagers did say, just before we burnt their shieling."

He saw Mara's shadow rear and tense. Sudden fear for her clogged his throat. He knew her now, could virtually sense the rash will that took hold of her from time to time. Would she be so mad as to rush out there, filled with indignation?

As silently as possible, he scooted toward her, the sound covered by that of the conversation which continued on the shore of the lochan.

"You should ha' led us to a brothel. 'Tis what I need this night."

Diarmad peered over Mara's shoulder at the scene beyond, silvered by starlight. Four men, all on horseback and most definitely not soldiers. Renegades, then, and as a sinister glitter revealed, all heavily armed. But what sort of renegades claimed the luxury of horses?

Mara turned her head and looked at him. Wide eyes conveyed her dismay and alarm, but she pressed her lips together and did not speak. She had no need to; her expression conveyed all. Were they safe beneath the pine boughs? If they remained silent, would they escape discovery?

He touched her arm for reassurance, and raised the sword in his hand, trying to convey his intent to fight for her—to the death, if need be. He did not know what manner of men these were, but four did not make impossible odds. And, he discovered with some surprise, he would shed the last drop of his blood for this woman.

The men at the shore of the lochan went on talking, jibing and challenging one another.

"You remember that time wi' the wee lass near Callander? How many times did we each tak' her before we were done?"

"Before she was done, daft cow. I do no' ken why she greeted and screamed so. What's a woman made for, save rutting?"

"Plenty of women left alone in their shielings now, since yon battle. Ripe for the plucking. Why do we have to chase this one?"

"Aye, 'tis accursed cold this night."

"Fools! This is more than just a woman. Those folk back there said she guides an important personage away from the battle. Do ye no' ken what that means?"

"It means you are chasing boogies through the heather when I stand in need of a warm bed."

"Aye, and if her charge is who I think he is, we need preserve only him and not her—she can warm your blood right enough, once we catch them."

Mara shuddered beneath Diarmad's hand, and he heard the breath catch in her throat. But the conversation beside the lochan went on.

"My nose tells me she is close by. Hiding,

mayhap."

Damn the fellow's nose anyway. Diarmad swallowed a groan, and Mara stiffened as her alarm increased.

"Light a torch, Neal, and we will look about. You follow that nose o' yours."

"Sweet heaven," Mara breathed.

"Whisht!" Diarmad exhaled into her ear.

He thought furiously. How well-concealed was their shelter? He had put it together with an eye to comfort and warmth rather than obscurity. Now surely no more than fifty paces separated them from the men. He began to sweat as he weighed their chances of remaining hidden and found them sorely lacking. All a searcher might need was light. If they lit that torch…

He would fight them, och, aye. But if they took him down, what would happen to Mara? Naught to the good, and that meant she would do better to escape.

The men below dismounted and began moving about; one of them struck a flame, and under cover of the distraction Diarmad whispered to Mara, "List to me, I want you to run. Do you hear me? Head up the hillside into the darkness and find cover. Promise me, now."

Once again she turned her head and gazed into his eyes. What did he see by the pale starlight? A world of emotion brimming over.

"Nay, I will no' leave you," she breathed.

"You must. You heard what they said. I will stay and engage them, give you every chance to get away. But you maun run like a hind, lass. 'Tis the best hope I can give you."

"Nay," she said again before bending forward and

pressing her mouth to his.

Aye, and even at such a moment as this her kiss seared him to the tips of his fingers and toes. All the emotion he'd seen in her eyes—that he could not quite identify—came rushing at him in a torrent. He felt her protest, her denial, and so much more.

Diarmad's heart, already racing, began to pound in his ears like a big, deep drum. Only his fear on her behalf caused him to push her away and steady her. "Promise me," he insisted.

Before she could answer, light flared at the edge of the lochan. The sudden radiance caused both Diarmad and Mara to stare. Diarmad's heart tripped in his chest; there beside the lochan lay something revealed by the light, something he could not identify. But the men fell on it like ravaging crows.

"I told you she was near! Is this no' a woman's shawl?"

In agony, Mara lamented, "By heaven, I maun have dropped it in the dark…"

"Hush," Diarmad told her and raised his sword before him. As he saw it, he had but one choice. He would not hesitate to buy her safety with his own.

"Come out, come out and play, wee lass! We ken fine you are here." The call came mockingly from the loch side.

Diarmad started forward, but Mara threw both her arms around him.

"Nay!"

All the renegades' heads swiveled toward her, as one.

"We hear ye, lassie!" In a body, the four men, with the one in the lead carrying a torch, moved toward them.

Diarmad's heart plummeted sickeningly. No time now for Mara to run. He shoved her behind him and told her fiercely, "Follow my lead."

He sprang up out of the shelter and to his feet. For an instant everything froze. The man in the lead, torch in his hand, halted. Diarmad fingered the hilt of his sword but did not raise it—not yet.

After a measured moment, the leader spoke. "Well, now, what have we here?" In the garish light, Diarmad saw the man grin. "Is it a cockerel?"

"Nay," Diarmad said as imperiously as he could manage in his bare feet, "it is your Prince."

****

Shivering with alarm and cold in the chilly air, Mara stared incredulously. What had the Ramsay just said? Had he gone mad entirely?

"Our what, do ye say?" the villain facing them demanded.

Swiftly, Diarmad returned, "Do you not know your rightful Prince, Charles Edward Stuart?"

Mara hissed between her teeth. The Ramsay almost made it sound convincing, for his voice—haughty and disdainful—held a note of command.

The other three men had paused behind their leader. "What is that?" cried one of them. "Who did he say he is?"

Their leader grunted. "Just as I thought. Your Highness," he stated mockingly, "I have had word of ye here about the countryside. Indeed, there is news of you having been seen all around the Highlands."

Mara could not see much of the man's face in the garish light, but his voice held a note of cunning.

"Those who ha' glimpsed your passing say you travel alone but for a lass."

"A brave lass," Diarmad concurred, "under my protection and in service to her King."

So that was what the Ramsay was about! Mara caught her breath again. If he hoped to appeal to these scoundrels' better natures—or their fealty—she feared the worst.

"And," Ramsay went on, "are you likewise brave men? Did you fight at the battle not long past and shed blood for my father—and me?"

"We may ha' raised our swords there," the leader said in a measured tone.

One of the others interrupted to jeer, "You are a fool, Neal. That is no' Charles Stuart."

"Well, now," the leader—Neal—said, "do no' be so certain." His narrowed gaze, quick in the torch light, gave Ramsay a closer inspection. "The Prince was hastened away out o' that furious battle, was he no'?"

"Aye, mebbe, but what would he be doing out here wi'out guards or any comforts?"

"Running like a fox," Neal replied. "Unfortunately for you, Your Highness, you ha' run straight into our hands. Pull your lass out o' there and let us take a proper look at her."

Ramsay lifted his head. "I will not. As I tell you, she is under my protection as well as that of my father's crown, and I will do as I must to protect her."

The men stirred, and Neal grinned disconcertingly. "You mean to engage us, sir? I do not think you will find any of us reluctant to shred your royal hide. Yet you are worth far more alive than dead. For her life, though, you will need to bargain."

Mara closed her eyes in agony. With what did Ramsay have to bargain? She feared herself doomed—she would be used by these scoundrels before her throat was slit, and Ramsay would be forced to watch. Worse, her father and Robert would never know what had happened to her. And she would never have another chance to kiss Diarmad Ramsay…

Carefully, she eased the *skean dhu* Robert had given her from the pouch at her side. Aye, well, she would not go easily, so they would find.

"I did no' see you, sir, at Culloden field," said one of the men at Neal's back unexpectedly, "but I was there at Glenfinnan when the clans were raised. For all the good that did any of us."

Aye, so, Mara thought. Diarmad Ramsay was not the only Highlander disillusioned with the cause.

Ramsay turned his face toward the man. "Then you saw me there—and you will recognize me now."

The man said nothing in the leaping torchlight.

Ramsay altered his tone. "List to me. I know well how many brave men fought and died—for my father's Cause and mine. We both owe the people of this country a debt we can scarce repay. That does no' mean I can let you abuse a woman under my protection."

Neal waved the torch for emphasis. "I would like naught better than to see Your Highness take on these rogues at my back. A prince fighting in defense of a peasant lass! What a story 'twould be to tell round a fire. But if you be who you claim, I can take no such chances. Accompany us quietly, Your Highness, and I give you my word the woman will come to no harm." He glanced at his men. "Archibald will want to see them, and that means you will ha' to forego your rutting, my lads, for the time."

That prompted a chorus of protest and grumbling, all of which Neal ignored. Mara scrambled to her feet at Ramsay's side, aching to reach for his hand, and slid her knife back into her pouch. It seemed they would live a while longer. But for better or worse, she could not tell.

Chapter Ten

"Those are Sassenach boots you are wearing," said the tallest man of the group to the Ramsay as they moved along. He walked at the side of his own mount, which he had surrendered to Diarmad; he guarded Mara, who walked also, as the dawn strengthened around them.

Mara had learned the tall man's name was MacBain, and she detested him most of the four. Reeking of sweat and with his hair hanging in a filthy tangle, he walked far too near for her comfort and kept shooting her lascivious glances. She could not imagine the horror of being forced by him.

But Ramsay stood between her and such a fate—Ramsay and Robert's *skean dhu*, now secreted in her skirt.

She spoke up before Diarmad could. "You will address His Royal Highness as 'Your Highness,' you great heathen."

MacBain turned an ugly stare on her. Aye, the morning light showed her far more than she wanted to see of both him and his companions. Possibly mercenaries, they went heavily armed and roughly clad. Their faces betrayed a hard mercilessness that terrified her.

MacBain raised a fist as if to strike her. "I will no' be corrected by a woman, even the Prince's trollop—if he is the Prince. I am no' convinced."

Ramsay shifted his mount toward them. "You will not touch a hair of her head. Do you understand?"

MacBain sneered. "Och, I hear ye, great Prince."

"Come on, and do no' play the fool," Neal chided MacBain. "Be he the Prince or one of his agents, he will be worth something. And we deserve a braw reward after that rout back there."

MacBain fell obediently silent, and Ramsay bent a hard look on Mara. She took his silent message; she should hold her tongue. Aye, well, he did not know her very well if he believed that possible.

Sonorously, Ramsay said, "I appreciate your valor on the field, my good men—and my father shall hear of it as soon as I return to France. Meanwhile, thank you for escorting me."

Aye, and where had Ramsay acquired that cultured voice? His own musical, Highland accent had nearly disappeared. Mara did not know if that was the way Charles Edward spoke in conversation, but it made a damned fine representation.

She eyed him sitting his mount with an air of natural hauteur. The Ramsay had untold depths.

The man called Marcus snorted in his turn. "Your father the king was supposed to make things better for Scotland."

"And he will."

"Could no' tell it by yon battle, could ye?" Marcus returned.

"The battle—despite your valiance and that of all the Scotsmen who stood for us there—did not go as planned."

"And now your royal whatsit finds yoursel' haring

about the heather wi' a wee lass. How's that meant to further this grand Cause o' yours?"

Mara drew breath to speak, and Ramsay glared at her again. "My advisors say this is the safest way to move me about the country. Obviously they did not count on your eagle eyes."

"Or Neal's nose," one of them jibed irreverently. Mara still could not tell just what they did, or did not, believe.

"Your Highness," MacBain pressed, "you still ha' no' explained why you are wearing Sassenach boots."

Damn those boots anyway, Mara thought viciously. She had told Ramsay to continue in the fine ones that had been procured for him.

"Mine were ruined departing the battle," Ramsay said loftily. "One of my aides gave me these."

"Would he no' ha' been more likely to give you his own boots," the first man asked, "rather than they that had been on the stinking feet of a damned Englishman?"

"His boots did not fit, and we were in extremis."

"Extremis!" the man repeated, and they all exchanged looks. "Cursed if he is no' the Prince, wi' words like that in him."

Neal said, "He is wearing the Stuart tartan and that fine doublet."

"Aye," agreed the first man, "and look at that sword! Spanish steel, I do not doubt, and finer than what we have."

"Come, Your Highness," Neal urged, "let us hasten on."

****

By the time they reached the renegades' base

camp, Mara felt ill with anxiety. The place, high on the steep slope of a narrow glen, comprised a cave and the area just beyond. Men came pouring out when Neal gave a whistle, and Mara's heart sank violently.

Could their situation be worse? Well, aye; Ramsay—His Highness—still stood between her and a fate truly more terrible than death. But for how long?

She shot a look at him and saw he yet retained his air of haughty confidence. How? Her own heart pounded so hard it shook her whole body.

At the head of the emerging men stood one—big and burly—who wore an assortment of tartans in scraps that looked to have been scabbed together, making it impossible to determine his clan of origin. A mane of flaming red hair overtopped it all, and he wore the expression of an angry Highland bull.

A chill chased its way up Mara's spine. At this man's mercy, they lay in true peril.

"What ha' we here, Neal MacNeal?" he called as they approached.

Neal called back, "'Tis himself—His Exalted Highness, Prince Charles Edward Stuart!"

Mara felt Ramsay, who had dismounted and stood beside her, stiffen. How it must gall him, being forced to play the part of the man he despised.

"What, then?" the red-haired bull called back.

"Charles Edward, wanted all over the Highlands! I thought we might just as well hold him for ransom."

Mere moments saw them seated in the dismal splendor of the cave, apparently the red-haired bull's fortress. Ramsay had been afforded a throne, built from stacked firewood, where all the bandits gathered around. Mara no longer doubted they were bandits. The things they had stolen lay scattered everywhere, along with their bedrolls, weapons, and enough dirt to make her want to pinch her nose.

She could not begin to guess how many bandits there were. She had tried to count, but terror blurred her vision and stopped her throat. Ramsay no longer need warn her to stay silent.

For his part, she could not guess from whence he garnered his composure. He occupied his rough throne like a prince true born and looked down his handsome nose at everyone impartially.

Still, not one of the bandits had made an obeisance. Of course, this lot probably would not bother to bow to their rightful king.

"I am Archibald," announced the bull, who sat on a plaid opposite Ramsay. "Your Highness will no' ha' heard of me, but I am a man of some renown in these parts."

"Are you a soldier, sir?" Ramsay returned serenely.

A laugh traveled round the group. "We fought at yon battle just past—or yon massacre, as it should better be called—and afterwards we gained a fortune stealing from the dead."

Ramsay wrinkled his aristocratic nose. "You are, then, an outlaw."

"Men do as they must to survive, Your Highness. You, living all comfortable in France, would ken little of that."

"But I assure you, I do." Ramsay lifted his chin. "My father has wept for the plight of his beloved people."

"Has he!"

"It is why he sent me here."

"Aye? And not, as we might suspect, out of sheer desire for the throne?"

"Desire, my man, has nothing to do with this undertaking."

Mara, standing at Ramsay's left shoulder, began to sweat. Despite his clever tongue this did not go well. She wondered fleetingly if she would ever get out of this dreadful place and see the sky again.

"Your arrogance argues you may just be who you say."

"Arrogance?" Ramsay repeated the word, sounding outraged.

"We heard him speak some high and mighty words," Neal put in.

"Did ye now? Still and all, if you are the Prince—Your Highness—you will ha' a ring or some other means of identifying your royal personage."

Would he? Mara froze where she stood. Laird Elliot had not thought of that.

Blandly, Ramsay said, "It, like all other things that might mark me, was removed from my person when I was smuggled away—for my own safety."

Archibald's shrewd gaze moved to Mara's face and back to Ramsay. "Your royal minders sent you off wi' but a slip of a lass?"

"No, my good man; with her and her brother. He was killed during an encounter south of here when we met a troop of English soldiers."

"My condolences, mistress." Archibald tipped his head at Mara, but she still could not tell whether he believed anything Ramsay said. "You have had a difficult time, have you not, Your Highness? That terrible defeat on the field, living rough on the hillsides, and now capture."

"Capture?" Ramsay stiffened.

Neal spoke up. "At least, Archie, he's had the comfort of a bonny lass all along the way."

"Aye, a warm pair of thighs is a boon to any man, be he royal or otherwise. Your Highness, I am thinking there will be a price on your head."

Ramsay flushed with what looked like indignation. "You would not think of betraying me to the English Crown. Not when you stood loyal with me at the battle just past?"

"While I hate to crush Your Highness's great and touching faith in us, we stood at the battle only for our own gain. Of course we hoped at the time you would prove victorious."

"Indeed?"

"That way we could steal from dead Sassenachs rather than fellow Scotsmen. But as I ha' pointed out, survival is survival. You shall be held wi' all due courtesy while we make inquiries as to your current value. Your wench—"

"My guide," Ramsay broke in imperiously, "is to remain unmolested."

MacBain spoke. "Why should Your Highness ha' the comfort of a woman while we ha' none? Will Your Royal Highness no' share?"

Ramsay rose to his feet, placing himself between Mara and MacNeal. "Have you no decency?"

"Very little, Your Highness," Archibald answered. "As you will soon see for yourself."

Chapter Eleven

"I am sorry I got you into this." Tears clogged Mara MacIvor's voice, making the words damned near indistinguishable. Ramsay's heart plummeted within him. He hated hearing evidence of her fear even more than he hated their wretched predicament.

Captured. Stripped of their weapons and under guard. Archibald had placed them in a segregated area at the back of the cave, fitted out for their supposed comfort with a number of rugs and even a flagon of wine. But they had been afforded absolutely no privacy, and eyes remained constantly upon them.

What looked like far too much space—and a forest of swords—separated them from the cave mouth. Diarmad did not know how he would win their way free.

Mara shifted closer to him on the rug they shared, and her shoulder butted his. He wished he could put his arm around her, but with so many watching, he dared not.

He wished, too, he had taken advantage and made love to her when he had the chance. They would probably never have another opportunity in this world.

"Are we going to die?" she asked in a whisper, echoing his thoughts uncannily.

Most likely. If not at the hands of these ruffians, then at the hands of the English Crown when Archibald turned them over for the price on Charlie's head. They would kick their last at the end of nooses, for treason.

Diarmad figured if he could keep Mara MacIvor from being vilely ravished before that happened, he would do well.

With honesty he told her, "I do no' ken. We shall have to see how this plays out."

"You are doing a wondrous job of being the Prince."

"Am I?"

"Och, aye."

He turned his head; their eyes met, and he caught from her an unexpected frisson of arousal. Ah, but she only found him attractive because he pantomimed her hero.

She leaned still closer. "Do you suppose you could strike a deal wi' yon Archibald?"

"What sort of deal?" And with what did she expect him to bargain?

"You might promise him something—a captaincy in your army, perhaps."

"What army?" he returned acerbically.

"Well, but he seems like a man in pursuit of glory. Such an offer may tempt him and let us get away out of here."

Diarmad shook his head.

She cuddled closer so her hair brushed his cheek. "I fear I have a more pressing problem."

"What is that?"

She gave him a rueful look before dropping thick, reddish-brown lashes. "I need to relieve myself."

Aye, and that did make a dilemma. Diarmad shot another swift look around the cave. She could scarcely hope to perform that duty before so many eyes.

He got to his feet and called haughtily, "Hie, Master Archibald!"

Archibald, busy giving orders near the front of the cave, ambled over to them. "What is it, Your Highness?"

With as much indifference as he could muster, Diarmad said, "My companion needs to relieve herself. Please conduct her to the privy."

Archibald eyed Mara with suspicion. "Aye, well, Your Great Highness, the privy, as you deem it, lies outside, and I am afraid you are far too valuable for us to risk either of you traipsing about."

"Surely she holds little value to you." If Diarmad could persuade them to release Mara, that would be half his battle won. Why should she march to her death beside him? He leaned toward Archibald. "Why not just let her go?"

"What will that gain me?" Archibald's eyes narrowed.

"It would earn you my good will, which is far more valuable to you than she. Indeed, sir, were you and I to strike an agreement, it might benefit you beyond your imagining."

"Maybe so. But am I to let her go haring off to find the dregs of your army and bring them after me—if you are who you say? Nay, we will sit tight for a time, and perhaps you and I may bargain, once I ha' learned what price sits on your royal head. Meanwhile"—he turned and hollered, "Marcus, bring a piss pot for His Royal Highness and his wench!"

Mara now stood on her feet beside Diarmad, her cheeks flaming.

"Och, no," she whispered.

Diarmad did not see any other options. He stood stiffly, and a battered and far less than clean pot was brought and laid at his feet. A few chuckles echoed around the place.

Archibald inclined his head. "There you go, Your Highness. And be sure and inform me if your royal self requires aught else."

He stalked away. Diarmad looked at Mara and saw tears of humiliation in her eyes.

"I canno'," she whispered in agony.

"You will have to. Here—put it back against the wall." He shoved the pot there with his own foot, then snatched up a rug and held it before her, screening her from the rest of the room. "Behind this. No one shall see you but me. And I promise no' to look."

After another agonized stare she obeyed. In time, he knew, he would have to do the same.

He tried to keep his promise and turn his eyes away; in truth, her skirts screened most everything. He caught only a glimpse of a smooth, bared cheek before he forced his gaze to the floor.

He heard Archibald laugh. "There, lads, is something you will no' see every day—a wee Highland lass wi' a royal attendant!"

****

Mara came awake slowly, despair in her heart. It seemed the dark emotion had followed her into sleep, rendering it troubled and restless. She remembered waking again and again to the bustle that filled the cave, and then near silence.

Now she opened her eyes with a thudding heart. Daylight shone through the mouth of the cave, but it must be very early, as few of their captors had yet stirred. She lay on her side with her head pillowed on something that exuded warmth; with a shock she recognized it for Diarmad Ramsay's lap. He sat propped against the cave wall, which must be far from comfortable, and at the moment dozed with his eyes closed.

Aye, and how handsome he looked even with the dirt of their journey upon him, and his princely finery ruined. And how perilous his position! Her heart twisted in her chest with a raw, searing emotion she could not at once identify.

She hated to stir and disturb what few moments' peace he might snatch. Who knew what horrors the day ahead might bring? She also hated to move away from the warmth of his thighs, the protective feel of his arm lying across her back.

Suddenly she wished she need never stir more than a few steps from Diarmad Ramsay, all her life long.

The unbidden thought shocked her over again. She could not possibly let herself fall for the Ramsay. 'Twould be the worst folly to give him her heart.

And yet who could fail to love such a man? Bonny, braw with the sword, and bright with valor.

He is everything the Prince should have been.

She corrected herself hastily. He was everything Charles Edward no doubt was also. The Prince's minders could not let him risk himself in battle, or on the trail. They must have forced him from the battlefield when he would sooner have stood at the head of his men with a sword in his hand.

Even as this man who now cradled her had done.

Again emotion flooded her—not for her prince, but

for Ramsay. She knew without question he would do what he could to protect her. He might fail, but his honor would remain bright.

She wondered about his father, who had sworn him to uphold that honor, before dying, and of all the people behind him—his ancestors and his brother, who may or may not still be alive. She wondered about the beautiful Una. For she must be gey beautiful, to capture this man's heart.

Why even worry about such things when they might never more see the light of freedom, when Ramsay would possibly never see Una again?

That thought prodded her to stir in protest, and Ramsay instantly came awake. His hand slid up her back to her head and cupped it, his touch steadying and reassuring her.

"List," he whispered. "I have been thinking about escape."

Slowly she sat up and rested her tangled head close by his against the cold wall. In the dim light his eyes looked more gray than blue.

"Escape?" she returned incredulously.

"Yours, not mine." He drew a deep breath. "There is little hope for me."

And had he been pondering that all the night? Preparing to sacrifice himself for her, even though she had got him into all this?

She pressed closer. His arm came about her shoulders and drew her in tight.

"How?" she breathed.

"You are right; I will have to bargain with Archibald. Trade on his greed."

"'Twould seem so. But if there is a great price on

your head—?" The Prince's head, she meant. Archibald had sent MacNeal out last night to try and discover just that.

"I shall have to offer him more."

"Aye." Mara's voice betrayed her uncertainty.

"Most important," he went on, "is keeping you out of their hands meanwhile. For I fear they would pass you from one to the other of these blackguards."

Mara's gaze moved among the "blackguards," most of whom still slept, and she shuddered inwardly. She counted nearly a score of them.

She would likely not survive such an ordeal or, if she did, not with her mind intact.

"Would they dare? I mean, if they think I belong to their Prince—"

"I ha' been thinking about that also. Yon MacNeal has gone out searching for word of the Prince. What if he finds it?"

"Eh?"

Ramsay lowered his voice until it became a mere breath that tickled Mara's ear. "Presumably the true Prince must be somewhere about the Highlands. If they get word of him—say, he has been captured elsewhere—there is no hope for us."

Mara contemplated that unpalatable truth. "Och, hell." These brigands, believing themselves deceived, would slaughter him and use her for their pleasure. "What chance have we?"

"Our only chance, as I see it," he told her, "lies in being even more cunning than yon Archibald."

Chapter Twelve

Three days passed in an agony of waiting nearly as intense as that which had preceded Culloden. At least then Diarmad had the luxury of speaking with others of his father's men, his da and Cainnech, and had been free to move about. They had, in fact, marched all the way to England on an ill-fated attempt to launch an attack there, only to return exhausted, half-starved, and poorly armed.

The battle, he now saw, had been forecast for disaster. Still, he'd felt he had a purpose.

Now he found himself doomed to sit, watching those who watched him, and worry—that and play the part of the bloody prince, which only became more and more a strain. How might the true Charles Edward behave in this situation? Would he issue orders, fall into a snit, give way to despair? For the life of him, Diarmad could not tell.

So he maintained an air of lofty, forced forbearance and provided Mara what little comfort he might. She grew more and more edgy with the passing time, and he feared her temper frayed dangerously.

And who could blame her? Unbound, they still inhabited a cage with invisible bars. Their pen seemed to consist of the space occupied by the rugs they had been given and not much beyond. If either of them attempted to stray, correction came swiftly in the form of grunts, rough gestures, or brandished weapons.

Aye, Diarmad got the point. They would not be harmed so long as they remained cooperative. At least, not yet.

"I shall go mad," Mara grumbled at him more than once. "Look how they stare at me."

So they did, the way starving men might look at fresh meat. But they approached only to bring food, water, or to swap out the piss pot that he and Mara, perforce, shared. At night, for comfort, she slept in his arms, and despite their situation he grew hard for her half the time.

Such forced intimacy, as he suspected, must forge a bond not unlike that between warriors in battle. That would explain why he felt so protective of her, willing to lay down his very life to spare her harm.

But she proved a trying, troublesome lass withal— her spirit rarely quiet, a tangle of emotions always in her eyes and with that restless energy in store. Keeping still so much of the time must be pure torment for her.

So far she had managed to let him, Diarmad, lead for both of them, even when Archibald approached with questions as he sometimes did. Then Mara fell back and sat by the wall while Diarmad lied as he might.

And lie he did—Archibald posed questions obviously thought up to trip him, requested details of the Prince's past life and future intentions. Diarmad manufactured replies with a facility that surprised him, reckoning that if he did not know the true answers, chances were neither would Archibald.

Once or twice Diarmad went on the offensive. "Tell me, Master Archibald, why you wear the tartans of so many of my faithful clans?"

Archibald looked down at himself. Bits and swatches of plaids fluttered about his great bulk; some had been roughly stitched together, some pinned in place. All were now filthy.

"These, Your Highness? A number belonged to men who served wi' me—for I was a true soldier once. Others, I took frae the men I killed. Those are the ones wi' blood on them."

It was no longer possible to tell which carried stains of blood. Diarmad looked Archibald in the eye. "And do you not wear the tartan of your own clan?"

"I do not, Your Highness. I ha' not that right, for I long ago betrayed those to whom I was born."

Now, late in the afternoon of the third day, Neal MacNeal returned. He came in out of a hard rain that had turned the cave damp and chill. Mara sat wrapped tight in one of the rugs, but she started up with the bustle at the cave mouth and seized Diarmad's arm.

"Look."

"I see."

MacNeal, well-wetted, shed his weapons and met immediately with Archibald, speaking furiously. Diarmad's heart sank in his chest. Clearly the man had found out something of importance. If he had word of the true Prince, Diarmad and Mara were surely doomed.

Archibald glanced toward them several times before placing a heavy hand on MacNeal's shoulder. Diarmad heard him say, "Get some whisky inside you, man. You ha' done well."

The focus of all eyes, Archibald then moved toward Diarmad and Mara. Diarmad met him on his feet, spine straight in defiance of the dread that seized him.

Archibald paused, balanced on the balls of his feet. "My man has just returned from Inverness, Your Highness, where there is word of you."

Behind Diarmad, Mara gasped. What word? Captured? Departed for France? Either would prove disastrous.

Archibald went on, "The Jacobites, it seems, are no longer singing in the streets of Inverness. And your rebellion is dead."

Diarmad looked him in the eye. Deliberately, he said, "How can that be, so long as I yet live? There are too many loyal hearts in Scotland yet."

Archibald snorted. "There is also a price on your head, Your Highness, of thirty thousand pounds sterling."

An unheard of sum! But Diarmad struggled to appear disdainful. Charles Edward would no doubt deem it his just worth.

He raised his chin. "None of my loyal subjects will betray me for that."

"You are wrong, Your Highness, for I will."

****

"What does it mean?" Mara, cuddled close to Ramsay's side, breathed the words into his ear. Since MacNeal's return, Archibald had posted an armed guard nearby, and she wanted them to overhear nothing.

Ramsay shook his head. "The Prince is still alive— and most likely still in flight."

So, Mara thought, Laird Elliot's plan held true. For Archibald would hand Ramsay over to agents of the Crown believing him to be Charles Edward.

And Ramsay would die.

To be sure, she had always known it possible. In

the beginning she'd believed she was ready to sacrifice herself and him. But nay, she had not known Diarmad Ramsay then.

Had not cared for him.

Her heart began to pound in deep, heavy beats. Still uncertain about the veracity of that other word—*love*— she nevertheless knew she would throw herself to the wolves for Ramsay's sake, if it might do any good.

In this case, it would not.

"What hope have we?" she begged.

"Archibald will turn us in for the head price. I fear our run is over."

Much as Mara's heart protested it, she could not refute his words. They sat in Archibald's power, surrounded and with no weapons.

Ramsay turned his head and looked her full in the eyes. "You ha' been a brave and true companion, Mistress MacIvor."

Tears flooded her eyes. "Och, I am so sorry—"

A rueful smile twitched his lips. "I do have one regret—that I did not lie wi' you when I had the chance."

Mara promptly went breathless. Desire rose in a staggering wave.

"I promise you, Your Highness, if we get away out of this 'tis the first thing—the very first thing—we will do."

"Ah, an added encouragement." For an instant the raw desire in his eyes matched her own.

"Listen, you must find a way to bargain with him, as you said before."

"Aye, but what can I give him worth thirty thousand pounds sterling?"

"I do no' ken. Whatever you must. A vast holding, perhaps? Something to elevate him."

"Aye, that might serve. He has set himself up as a bandit laird—perhaps he would take the bait of a promised grand estate."

For several moments Ramsay fell silent, though Mara sensed he thought furiously. "But for all his treachery, the man is no fool. The offer must seem genuine."

Mara spread her hand on Ramsay's chest and moved her palm across the muscles, just for the pleasure of touching him. Even at this moment, with danger all around, she could not keep from wanting him.

Below his breath he mused, "Difficult to tell, when I do no' ken from whence he has come or all of what he keeps for ambition."

"Still," Mara tipped into his ear, "he yet believes you are the Prince, so there is some hope."

"Aye. Hope," Ramsay repeated ruefully. "We shall see."

When morning came, the bandits arose with new purpose. Ramsay stood and watched as Archibald gave orders and his men bustled about in response. Mara realized he had already gleaned the truth. The bandits mobilized: Archibald meant to move them this day.

Sure enough, they were offered no breakfast, and Archibald approached as soon as the light streaming through the cave mouth strengthened.

"Good news, Your Highness! You will be leaving here today. Much as I have enjoyed having you as my royal guest, my agent Master MacNeal will take you south and see you safe into…other hands."

Ramsay's spine straightened, and he summoned up indignation worthy of Charles Edward himself. "You mean to betray me? For silver?"

"Aye." Archibald did not seem ashamed of it. "Like Judas himsel'."

"Would you so easily condemn your people and your rightful King?"

"My people? I have none—save perhaps this rabble you see gathered around you, and I would sell them also if I thought I could get a decent price. You, sire, will bring me a very decent price indeed and so will be the making of me."

"What of your honor, sir?"

Mara knew it for a futile question even before it fell from Ramsay's lips. Archibald had no honor and quite possibly no conscience.

"Honor?" Archibald repeated, as if he'd never heard the word, and accompanied it with a wave of his hand. "Get your royal self ready; you depart at once."

Ramsay turned; his eyes met Mara's in a speaking look. He must make his bid now, or not at all.

"Gather up your things," he told her, "while Master Archibald and I yet deal together."

"Ah—no," Archibald objected quickly, and they both turned to stare at him. "The lass will no' be going wi' you."

"What?" Ramsay bellowed.

"I ha' decided to retain her—a wee prize in return for your keep, Your Highness. You are to leave, but she stays."

Chapter Thirteen

"Unacceptable," Diarmad snapped. Rage rose to his head in a powerful surge. He did not lose his temper often; Cainnech had schooled him far better. A man who lost his head made himself vulnerable. But at this moment outrage sought to overthrow common sense. "I am responsible for this woman's safety, and I find that a sacred trust. I will not leave her behind."

Archibald eyed him with a new expression in his eyes. "Spoken like a true Highlander—sire. Perhaps you show your Stuart blood."

That set Diarmad back on his heels. In his anger, had more of his Highland brogue emerged? He could not afford to give himself away now when only his status stood to protect Mara.

"But," Archibald went on, "I am afraid I do no' believe in sacred trusts. She stays wi' me."

"Listen here—my good man." Diarmad narrowed his eyes and stepped forward, struggling to keep his persona in place. "I will buy her safety from you, if that is what you require."

Archibald gave him a look of surprise. "With what? I already have the coin pouch with which you arrived."

"Stealing from your monarch—have you no shame?"

"Save your breath, Your Highness. We ha' already

established I have no honor. No shame, either. What would you offer me?"

Diarmad set himself and drew a breath. "Your own kingdom."

"Eh?" Archibald cocked his head. "What is that you say?"

Those around them now eavesdropped shamelessly, including Neal MacNeal, who stood several paces behind Archibald.

Diarmad no longer cared. He waved an arm at the cave. "You set yourself up here as a lord of the hills, ruling your holding with an iron hand. But what, in truth, do you possess? I am willing to offer you a holding worthy of your ambitions."

Archibald's eyes narrowed and his expression turned avid. "Where?"

"Your own island," Diarmad proposed, "and a small fleet of ships for transport and defense."

The cave fell so silent Diarmad heard birds singing outside. For once, Archibald could find nothing to say.

Diarmad pressed his advantage. "It is the finest offer you will ever receive, far better than you can hope to get from the English Crown. Why, the king's agents are notorious for failing to deal honestly. You may well turn me over only to receive nothing in return and might find yourself taken into custody for questioning—or worse."

"Aye." Archibald must have considered that indisputable fact. It was the very reason why he would send Neal MacNeal in his place, as he now betrayed with a glance at that man.

MacNeal did not miss the significance of that pointed look and stiffened where he stood.

"What island, and where?" Archibald asked.

"The Hebrides. My father holds many such and will deed one to you in full, at my request."

"And the ships? I am no sailor."

"You have many men here who will have served beneath the sail. Only think, man, your own kingdom—a natural fortress. No one could take it from you."

Archibald thought on it. The watching men held their breaths.

"All you need do," Diarmad pressed, "is let me go free—along with my companion. A deed of fealty."

Diarmad then waited while Archibald considered, his fate—and, more importantly, Mara's—hanging in the balance.

But at length Archibald shook his head. "'Tis a handsome offer, sire, but too big a gamble for me. In order for me to be granted this kingdom of which you so generously speak, your father would need to regain the throne. And I am no' certain that will ever happen."

He turned and nodded at MacNeal. "Get ready. You leave at once."

****

From where she stood Mara could feel Ramsay's rage burning steady and bright. So far he had managed to keep a lid on it, but his handsome face looked white with strain as he gathered up his few belongings. He had made his best bid on her behalf—and lost. That did not mean he was done fighting.

Aye, for she began to know this man together with whom she'd been thrown, and his fierce, loyal heart. Honor burned bright in Diarmad Ramsay. He may have been constrained to this dangerous scheme—for it did seem mad and dangerous now, even to Mara—but he would not abandon her easily.

Yet the cave was full of Archibald's men, and Ramsay stood unarmed. What would happen to him if he tried to fight? Archibald, thinking him of value, might not kill him outright, but he might be sore hurt, and it would avail them nothing.

Mara must stay and he must go. They must part.

She could not stand it. Even more than fearing what would befall her once he had gone, she dreaded losing his company. Impossible that she might never see him again, catch the glint of humor in his eyes or the wry smile that often lit his face. Never have another chance to kiss those warm lips, lie close against his body, or feel his hands caress her flesh.

Breathless with panic, Mara stood trying to comprehend her pain; the truth that had dogged her for days would not be denied.

She loved this man to the root of her soul, and beyond.

Should she tell him? This would be her one and only chance, and it seemed important to do so, to spill the knowledge into his ears, make it his possession—as she now could never be. Yet their parting took place here before scores of eyes. She could not even move, as she wished, into his arms.

He drew himself up and looked at her. What did she see in his eyes? Regret? Desire? The anger still burned bright and seemed to consume the other emotions; she could not tell.

And they had only moments. Without using words, she must convey what she felt.

"Go safely, Your Highness." *It wounds me to the heart knowing I will never see you again.*

"You have been a good and faithful servant, mistress, a credit to your family and our Cause." *I do not want to leave you in these hands. I am sorry, sorry—*

"It was my honor, Your Highness. I would do it all again, even knowing the outcome." *I wish I could kiss you one last time, a strength against what is to come.*

"May God protect you." *Because I cannot.*

No thought for the fact that he, Diarmad Ramsay, went to his death even as she went to pain and shame. For Mara did not doubt he would be seized for treason as soon as MacNeal sought to turn him over to the English authorities for the ransom. Would she also be dead by then? Or would she but wish for death?

She sank into a curtsy and pressed her forehead against his hand, the only way she had to touch him.

"Very affecting," Archibald bellowed. "But we are wasting time. Come, sire—or would you prefer I send the English king your head?"

Ramsay ignored him and, in defiance of custom, drew Mara up into his arms. For an instant he pressed her to his heart and breathed into her ear, "I will no' leave you in their hands. I will return for you—I swear it!"

"Come, sire—the horses await."

Ramsay released Mara, turned away, and without a backward look followed Archibald and MacNeal from the cave.

Chapter Fourteen

He had gone. Once the truth of that penetrated Mara's shock, devastation took her to her knees again. She sank down onto one of the rugs they had shared in their makeshift prison, like a woman slain.

No one so much as glanced at her; life in the cave went on. Men bustled around, and Archibald came back into the cave to sit upon his rough throne. The bright sunlight continued to stream in, and only the sound of hoofbeats beyond the cave mouth marked Ramsay's departure.

Mara wondered if she'd ever be out in that warm sunlight again or if she would die in this damp, cold place once they battered her to pieces.

He said he would return.

She wondered when her horror and torment would begin. Did Archibald mean to take her first? Kneeling there with her fingers covering her face, she shuddered. And when he finished would he pass her to the rest of his men? Either way she would not—could not—survive long.

Ramsay swore he would rescue me. Mara's whole heart strained toward that promise and her belief in the man behind it. But how? He was himself a prisoner and destined for the noose or the block. Yet she could live a while longer if she placed her faith in him.

She pressed her eyes shut, and a vision of Diarmad

Ramsay arose in her mind: his handsome, haughty face, his mobile, clever mouth, the regal nose she loved to admire, and those eyes, so often full to brimming with his thoughts be they courageous, impatient, or flaming with desire. She must hold to that image, as to a glimmer of light in darkness, and let it sustain her through the ordeal to come.

For he had said he would return for her. She had no idea how, yet she did believe. And that meant when he came she had still to be alive.

And waiting.

****

"Where are you taking me?" Diarmad struggled to keep his assumed accent in place while seeking to discipline his emotions. Leaving Mara MacIvor in the hands of those villains and walking from the cave hurt like a physical wound. Nine parts of his attention and all his heart lay back there with her. But for her sake he could not afford to make a mistake.

"Just you let me worry about that, sire," MacNeal replied.

Diarmad narrowed his eyes against the shock of bright daylight after the thick gloom of the cave. The day—one of those that sometimes graced the Highlands in spring with clear, blue skies and sweet air—could not be bonnier. He gazed about and furtively tried to ascertain his location. He and Mara had been traveling north by northwest when they stumbled upon the lochan. He thought Archibald's men had taken them southwest from there. Some distance west of Inverness, then.

He eyed his companions, a party of four. MacNeal led the way, an inscrutable look on his face. The other three ranged around Diarmad, one to the rear and one at either hand, all heavily armed. He had no weapon.

If he had, he might attempt a fight—throw himself at the man on his right, startle the other horses, and begin a fray. His anger over what could be happening even now back in the cave, his grief at leaving Mara, pressed him to it. If he'd had so much as a *skean dhu*…

Likely he would get but one chance to surprise them; he dared not waste it.

Sickness roiled in his gut. He thought of the look in Mara MacIvor's eyes when he left her: wide, haunted, full of fear and another emotion that had stopped his breath.

By God, he had never known a woman with such a courageous heart. Her spirit rode with him yet, both a comfort and a torment.

He cared so much for her.

That thought surprised him even as he acknowledged it. How had it happened, and when? He did not agree with her way of thinking or her foolish loyalties. Moreover, he'd believed his heart irrevocably if hopelessly entrusted to Una's keeping—mysterious, unattainable Una, with her fall of ebony hair and the secrets in her eyes. She never would disclose the truth of how she felt about Cainnech…and him.

He would not find out now, never behold the hills of home, and likely not gaze into Una's beautiful face.

Strange how that thought caused no twinge, while his heart strained back toward the woman he had just left. He must survive, if only to succor her.

That would be his battle cry.

****

"A word, sire."

They had stopped for a brief rest, their first since leaving Archibald's cave early that morning. Diarmad, on his own feet at last, prepared himself for action and weighed his chances. One of Archibald's men tended the horses near the stream. The two others appeared to stand guard. MacNeal, that unreadable look still on his face, approached Diarmad softly.

Clinging hard to his role, Diarmad turned his face away. "I do not engage in conversation with traitors. That is what you are. In turning me over to the Crown, you engage in the highest form of treason."

"Well, now, Your Highness, that is a matter of opinion. According to many, the treason lies all on your side—inciting a rebellion against your king."

Diarmad glared at the man, letting his anger show; it did not take much effort. "My father is your rightful King, as any true Scotsman would affirm."

MacNeal stepped closer still, so near Diarmad could smell the sweat on his clothes. "Happen I agree with you."

That caught Diarmad's attention. What was this? A glimmer of hope?

He closed his lip, assumed a royal stance, and waited.

"But a man has to survive, see," MacNeal went on. A strange, troubled expression came to his face. "Long ago, when first I left home, sire, I would ha' followed you without hesitation. I am sure my former clansmen stood strong and fell bravely on the field in your service."

"But you are not in my service now. Instead you would deliver me into chains. You disgrace those who birthed you."

MacNeal did not so much as blink. "As I say, sire, a man maun get by in this harsh world. I ha' worked my way up to Archibald's second-in-command. The thing is—"

"Yes?"

"I would like to be first in command." MacNeal leaned still closer and lowered his voice. "Does that offer you made to Archibald still stand?"

"Eh?" Surprise nearly made Diarmad forget his role.

"The island, sire, and the fleet o' ships. Would you offer all that to me?"

For one brief instant, a terrible surge of combined shock and hope rendered Diarmad mute. The answer to prayer was this. And Charles Edward would no doubt think such allegiance his due. Diarmad struggled hastily to reassume that persona and gave a lofty nod.

"I would—and I do so offer it to you, MacNeal. As soon as I am free, I will get my father's writ upon it. You shall be a lord of the isles, and no one will be able to gainsay you."

MacNeal's eyes blazed with desire.

"But," Diarmad pressed quickly, "we must go back and rescue my wee guide. It is a matter of honor with me. I do not leave behind those who serve me." *Except all those on Culloden's bloody field, torn and broken— including one Chief of Clan Ramsay with his stubborn, loyal heart.*

MacNeal gaped at him. "Impossible! We are already clean away. And 'tis but the four of us against Archibald's lot."

"Five, if you will arm me. We rescue her, MacNeal, or there will be no deal between us."

MacNeal's eyes narrowed. "Servant is she, or your royal doxie?"

Diarmad decided to appeal to the man on a level he could understand. "A little of both. But it is my honor at stake, MacNeal, as I have said. I would no sooner abandon her than this promise I make to you." Intently he said, "You wish me to keep my word in that, do you not?"

"Aye, but, well, sire, she will no doubt be hard-used by now anyway, and no good to you."

Diarmad's heart plummeted. "Do you suppose that villain Archibald will have had her already?"

"Maybe. He will take her first, but when he is good and ready. These days the old stoat maun work up to it."

"We must turn back at once, then, and ride hard. If you want your reward."

Pure greed gazed at Diarmad from MacNeal's eyes. "I do."

"Good man. Can you persuade your companions?"

"I chose them wi' just this idea in mind. If I offer them a share, I believe they will come along."

"Then let us move at once. And by God, give me a sword!"

Chapter Fifteen

How much time had passed? Mara found it impossible to guess. The bright patch of sunlight at the front of the cave had faded, which meant the day grew older. No one had come near her even to offer food or drink, or to empty the piss pot. All those attentions must have been aimed at Archibald's royal captive.

Whatever the cause, Mara could only be grateful. Archibald remained occupied, speaking with certain of his men, and did not so much as turn his eyes in her direction.

Where was Ramsay now? Just thinking of him made her heart ache with hope and longing. She did not doubt he would come, but would he be in time?

It seemed not. For now, in what had to be late afternoon, Archibald at last turned his attention to her, stirred, and heaved his great bulk to his feet, adjusting the front of his kilt significantly.

Mara, crouching against her bit of wall, could not take her eyes from him. She followed him the way a bird might watch a tomcat as he made his way across the cave and paused in front of her.

"Well, now, lass—'tis time for me to take the price of your keep."

Everyone in the cave—at least six men—stared. Was this terrible thing to happen before their eyes, then? Mara's gut churned, and heat stained her skin.

Would no one intervene to help her? Nay, for they no doubt awaited their chances.

"Please, no," she said. She had never begged for anything, but terror made her all too ready to do so now.

"Come, lass, you canno' expect me to forego my due. I ha' never gone where royal flesh has gone before me."

"It did not; we did not," Mara stammered. "I was no' with the Prince that way."

Archibald cocked his head. "You think I believe that? A lovely wee piece like yoursel' alone wi' him on the hillside… Do you take me for a fool?"

"Nay, not at all. But the Prince held me in far too much respect—"

Archibald laughed, not a reassuring sound. "Unfortunately for you, lass, I ha' no respect for anyone, save mysel'. You will warm me this night, and if I find you pleasing, tomorrow as well."

Mara's desperate gaze stole to the mouth of the cave.

"Do you truly expect him to turn up and save you—that royal Jessie? He will be half way to captivity by this time." Archibald began to hitch up his kilt. "Best be pleasing now, or I will let my men ha' you."

Mara squeezed her eyes shut, turned her face to the stone wall, and began to pray. She did not want to see what Archibald kept under his kilt, could not imagine him touching her. Her heart beat against her ribs like a bird in a cage.

But the prayer seemed to avail her nothing. Archibald lowered his great bulk with a grunt and seized her by the ankle. She smelled him then, a reek of sweat and aging unwashed male that turned her stomach violently.

His hand closed on her other ankle, and he pulled her from the wall toward him, her legs parted. Eyes still tight shut, every sense trying to block what must come, she attempted to steel herself.

"Hold!"

The cry came from the mouth of the cave and rent the rapt silence. Archibald grunted again and released Mara's ankles. Her eyes flew open.

She beheld an incredible sight. For Diarmad Ramsay, his hair flying, stood in the cave opening with a sword in his hand and men at his back.

In that first instant she saw only that—Ramsay agonized and determined, with his gaze reaching for her, the bright weapon in his hands and others behind him. She'd seen how he could fight with that weapon, and her heart buoyed up.

Yet the cave teemed with armed men. Had Ramsay come back for her only to meet his death?

Archibald heaved himself to his feet, and Mara stumbled up after. Archibald drew his weapon, a long knife he wore at his back.

"What is this, then?" he roared. "MacNeal, do you betray me?"

Only then did Mara realize the man directly behind Ramsay was indeed Neal MacNeal. She gasped. Had Ramsay managed to turn MacNeal's loyalty?

The expression on MacNeal's face said it all: glowering, defiant. He called out in reply to Archibald, "Why should you be the one offered a grand kingdom? You are no better than me."

"Am I not? We shall see about that!"

With a roar, Archibald charged—not Ramsay but MacNeal. It looked very like a bull attacking a whippet, but MacNeal stood firm, the sword in his hand outreaching Archibald's long knife.

No one else moved as the two met to battle, save for Ramsay, who took one prudent step aside before hurrying to Mara.

"Come."

"But we are surrounded." Mara stole another look around the cave even as she spoke. No one had attention to spare for her; all eyes had fixed on the two men who now bellowed at one another like enraged boars, even as steel met steel.

Ramsay clutched Mara's hand, and his desperate, determined gaze focused her. "Hurry."

A few eyes did flick to them as they edged along the wall of the cave toward the door. They pressed close by one bandit, who drew his weapon, and the breath stopped in Mara's throat. But the man's attention switched back to the combatants, and Ramsay urged Mara on.

MacNeal grated, "Archibald, your great prize is slipping away!"

"I will deal wi' you and then wi' him!" Archibald returned.

Ramsay leaped through the cave opening and dragged Mara with him. She found herself all at once in the light of late afternoon. The sunshine had disappeared in a raft of cloud, but it still hurt her eyes after so long shut away inside.

Ramsay gave her no time to recover. "Here, up wi' you." He lifted her bodily and placed her on one of the horses that stood in a cluster before he vaulted onto a second, caught her reins, and started away.

From within the cave behind them came a wordless roar. Mara spun about, almost unhorsing herself when her mount jerked into motion. What had happened? Had one of the combatants killed the other? Surely not so soon. And would the others now come after her and Ramsay? Two horses still stood in the gathering gloom, ready for pursuit.

She could not see Ramsay's face, just the back of his head and his shoulders stiff with intent. More sound blossomed in the cave, a great howling, but they did not stay to determine the cause.

Instead, Mara held on for her life as they negotiated the slope in front of the cave and took the scree at breakneck speed. No time for words; the wind whipped her face and tossed her hair into her eyes. She clutched her mount's neck with grim determination.

How long they went so, with Mara's heart beating up in her throat, she could not say. At the foot of the slope lay a stand of trees; Ramsay threaded his way between them and increased his speed when he came out the other side, heading roughly north.

At last his horse foundered, forcing him to slow. The beasts had already covered a lot of ground this day, and, with a fierce look behind, he halted in the shelter of a copse, deep beneath the boughs.

Almost before they stopped moving, he was on his feet at Mara's side.

"Are you all right?"

He reached for her, and she tumbled into his arms. Fiercely, he drew her in against his heart, the one place she wanted to be.

His breath gusted against her cheek. "He did no'—

they did no'—"

"You got there just in time." Mara closed her eyes against a powerful wave of emotion. "How did you get there in time?"

"Prayer."

"But how did you persuade MacNeal to turn?"

"His own greed did that job for me. Listen, they will be coming as soon as one of them kills the other. I am a fool."

"Eh?"

"I should have taken all the horses and left them no means to pursue us. I could think of naught but getting you away."

He pressed his lips to her temple. She lifted her face and gazed into his eyes.

Blue-gray eyes, bright in the dull afternoon, they contained chagrin, determination, strength—and desire. They contained Mara's whole world.

She went breathless again, for a different reason. Time seemed to stop along with her heartbeat as she offered her parted lips.

And oh, the bliss of it, the sweet fire blazing to completeness as his mouth claimed hers. Surely she had been created for this sensation—his mouth on hers, his tongue stroking hers and then claiming her to her very soul. Her heart resumed beating like the wings of a bird in flight—for him, only for him.

When he broke the kiss, she wanted to weep. But he caught her face between his hands and gazed into her eyes again.

"Mara," he said, and it went through her like music. Her legs turned to water beneath her, and she trembled.

"Diarmad. I knew you would come for me." Her eyes filled with tears. "I did no' ken how."

All at once she wept against him, cuddled into his chest, and he let her cry while making soft, soothing sounds in his throat. It did not go easily with Mara to admit fear, but the ordeal just past had shaken her beyond telling.

After a few moments he wiped her face with gentle hands and kissed the last of the tears away. Tenderness flared at once to passion. Mara wanted this man, his hands upon her flesh, the strong length of him filling her, as she had never wanted anything.

But she scarcely supposed this made a proper setting, with pursuers behind them and danger all around.

Reluctantly, she drew away far enough to speak. "What now?"

He looked around. The Highland sun had already dipped toward the horizon, and rain threatened.

"Now," he said, "we find a good place to hide."

Chapter Sixteen

"We dare not have a fire," Diarmad told the lass beside him. They sat together in the dell he had found half way down the glen—a place just large enough to conceal them and both horses. He only hoped he'd left no trail behind.

It did not matter which of the men—Archibald or MacNeal—won the combat back there. The other would come after them, and the result would be the same. Diarmad had very little with which to defend Mara MacIvor, naught but a single sword and every last drop of his blood. That might not be enough if their pursuers came in a swarm.

"Do you think they will be able to follow us?" Mara asked.

He had done his best to assure not. But MacNeal and his lot were able trackers who had trailed them before without Mara knowing; the bandits as a whole would be skilled in that regard. And he, Diarmad, had several times been forced to choose speed over caution.

"Quite probably," he admitted, hating to add to her dread. He could feel her weariness and despair as if they were his own. The lass had been shattered by her ordeal, the last of her considerable strength nearly gone.

They—and the horses—desperately needed a night of rest before running again.

He turned to Mara and laid his hand on her knee.

She sat so close beside him her shoulder butted against his. "You are certain they did no' harm you?"

She shook her head. Her wild hair made a nimbus around her face. "You say MacNeal's greed turned him?"

"He wanted for himself the kingdom I offered Archibald." He could deliver that kingdom to neither, which meant he must stay one jump ahead.

He pondered and tried to determine their location; at the moment he barely knew north from south. But he would have to set a course when morning came.

Meanwhile…meanwhile the night closed around them, the two horses dozed, and the way Mara MacIvor looked at him took his breath away.

"We will no' need a fire," she said, "if you keep me warm."

She moved still closer. Diarmad gathered her up and drew her across his knees, precisely where he wanted her.

"Mara," he said.

Their lips met without further persuasion, followed by their tongues. Raw need leaped within him, brighter than ordinary desire. He felt at once empowered and humble, as if he owned her and at the same time knelt at her feet. He wanted her beyond expressing, required her still more.

She moaned, and the sound further ensnared him. Time ceased to exist as they explored one another's mouths, the heat rising until Diarmad's heart pounded up in his ears, even as he grew hard below.

When at last she drew her mouth from his, he felt it like a physical loss, until she whispered, "We made one another a promise, as I recall, back in yon cave."

He gazed into her eyes, questioning. "Do you say, Mara MacIvor, you are willing to give yoursel' to me this night?"

"More than willing." She leaned forward and ran her tongue along his bottom lip before moving her warm, open mouth further down to his throat. Deliberately and shamelessly, she tasted him, ran her tongue still farther down and down until it encountered the hair on his chest.

"I ha' but one complaint, Diarmad Ramsay."

"What is that?" And how could he answer it? He felt as if his wits might fly clean away, leaving him in a welter of searing desire.

"You are wearing far too many garments." She followed each word with a little flick of her tongue. Diarmad had a sudden blinding vision of her hot mouth closing on him down below—or perhaps, as he prayed, it was a presentiment.

"Aye, well," he managed to croak, "you keep insisting I wear the cursed things."

"But I thought you detested them."

"So I do."

"Then by all that is holy, why have you no' shed them? I tell you, I caught a glimpse of you bare once, and I ha' never stopped wishing for it again."

"Is that so?"

"It is."

"And you, beautiful lass?" He brought his hand to her bodice and pressed the palm to her breast. The soft mound, delectable even through the fabric that covered it, felt lush and warm.

"Do as you will," she told him, "for on this night I am yours."

The breath hitched in Diarmad's chest, but he did not let that stay him. They might have but this one night before they faced capture and ultimate execution.

He must make it last, despite his damned impatience.

He unlaced her bodice slowly, with fingers that trembled, and the fabric parted to reveal two heavenly swells, white in the near darkness. His turn, now, to bend forward and run his tongue across her flesh. Aye, he had wanted this nearly every time she moved or he looked at her, but the taste of her outmatched all his imagining.

She lay back across his knees supported by his arm, his free hand still at her breast. Her wild hair spilled around her shoulders, and the cool air pricked her nipples into tantalizing peaks. Her eyes met his, full of emotions he scarcely dared identify. Lust? Surely. Love?

That possibility shook him to his heart, but he could not let it stay him now, not with plundering her on his mind. He bent to her again, and the last of his restraint flew away.

****

From the first moment she beheld him behind her family's burnt shieling, Mara had desired Diarmad Ramsay. All the while they journeyed together, even when they squabbled and disagreed, that desire had continued to ride her hard.

Not nearly so hard as she wished for Diarmad Ramsay's beautiful body to ride hers, now.

He had stripped the clothing from her slowly in the near dark, his mouth claiming each bit of skin he uncovered in turn. All the while he remained clothed, save for his open shirt where Mara planted her hands with unconscious claiming. The slow progression heightened her desire unbearably, lit her from within, and made her feel both powerful and vulnerable. She did not like relinquishing control, and the sensation confounded her, but cursed if she would leave go of him.

By the time he stripped off the last of her garments, she had been reduced to a state of quivering shamelessness. With her breasts still wet from his tongue, she parted her thighs and began to pray.

The sensation of his fingers sliding into her brought her to fever pitch. He fixed his bright gaze on hers as he entered her again and again, and she felt him like a rod of iron beneath her buttocks.

Why did he wait? She wanted that rod to replace those fingers. *Now.*

"Please," she whimpered.

"For what do you ask, Mara MacIvor?" His voice crooned at her out of the night.

"You."

He withdrew his fingers from her ready body, but only to pluck at one breast. She nearly reared up off his knees.

"Are you certain?"

Sweet heaven, if she were any more certain she would wrap her naked legs around his neck and get that clever mouth of his where she wanted it.

As if he heard her thoughts, he slid out from beneath her at last, but not to disrobe. Instead he gently parted her thighs further, bent his head, and answered her prayers.

And oh, by all that was holy—or unholy—she had

never conceived of such pleasure. His lips wooed her in the most intimate of kisses before he entered her with his tongue, and she ignited with bliss.

Och, and even her most daring dreams had not conceived of this. It certainly had not been this way with—ah, but she could no longer recall the lad's name, filled as she was with Diarmad, only Diarmad. Diarmad who now owned her body, and to whom she would willingly offer not only her flesh but her very life.

While still her mind quivered with pleasure, he withdrew and made his way up her body, dropping kisses as he came. When he reached her mouth, she seized him in a firm grip.

"Get those clothes off," she growled, "and fulfill your promise."

He laughed, which did powerful things to Mara's pulse. "I needed to taste you first. I ha' been imagining how you would taste, far too long."

"I hope I do no' disappoint."

"What do you think?" He kissed her deeply, open mouth to open mouth, and she tasted what he had tasted, tangy and potent. She knew no shame then, and no doubt. She tore at his clothes, her mouth still fastened to his.

He laughed again, breaking the kiss, and reared above her. Gaze holding hers, he shed his doublet and his sark, revealing magnificent shoulders. When his hands moved to his kilt, Mara stopped breathing. Who needed to breathe?

She had seen all of him behind the shieling, aye, but not in a state of arousal so flagrant it widened her eyes and turned her blood to liquid fire.

Helpless, she reached for him. "I want to taste you

also." Yet she did not know if she could wait to feel him inside her, filling and completing her.

And when he murmured, "Not just yet," she snared him with naked legs and drew him home.

Home. How could she even imagine that word in these straits? She had no home now, and he lay far from his. But as his body wooed her with power and sweetness, as he plunged into her again and again, that notion echoed and reechoed in her mind.

Until she shattered into a thousand pieces and lost the capacity to think at all.

How much time passed then, Mara could not tell. She came to herself slowly, awareness finding her in bits: first the sensation of his cheek against her breast, where it had come to rest, and his breath sweeping over her; next the fact that he remained still inside her, the two of them fused into something far greater than either of them could ever be, apart.

The scent of him, and their loving, enfolded her like the heat from his body, a heady perfume. His hair brushed her cheek, his fingers splayed across her belly.

And she still wanted him, just as fiercely as ever.

How could that be? After she had lain with Donald—ah, aye, that was his name—she'd been quite certain she never wished to do so again. But that had been a rough-and-tumble thing.

This… She had no words for what had just passed between her and Diarmad Ramsay, nor for the bright need that rode her yet, even with him still inside her.

He lifted his head slightly and gazed into her eyes, making her heart stutter in her chest.

"Well, Mara MacIvor, and did I keep my promise?"

"You did, Laird Ramsay, and quite well." She drew a breath that lifted him on her breast. "And, I hope, no' for the last time."

Chapter Seventeen

Diarmad awoke to the alluring sensation of Mara MacIvor's mouth moving on his skin. The sheer, staggering pleasure of it chased every sensible thought and all chances of further sleep from his head.

He opened his eyes onto darkness and wondered how much time had passed. Surely it could not be the same night when he had drawn her up across his knees and taken her for the first time, finding in her well of heat a belonging he had never imagined.

Nay, for she must have been in his life forever, and part of him.

But as his senses returned, he realized they lay in the small hollow he had located last evening, with the patient horses still standing beyond, he and Mara naked and fast in one another's arms. His mind stumbled over it as he tried to sort out all that had occurred: the flight from the cave, refuge, and then the sheer white heat of their intimacy.

Aye, he knew her now. He had tasted her just as she had tasted him—that memory held the power to stun him to the tips of his toes. It must be near morning, yet the dark still hung around them, and Mara's mouth became insistent.

Even as he came awake she freed herself from his arms and slid her lips down his body, lingering at shoulder, chest, and ribs. He felt the flick of her tongue,

119

followed by the brush of her wild hair, and just like that his desire came alight.

By the devil's eyebrows, how could he be aroused again, so soon? Yet so he did find himself, and his member stood strong for her when she reached it, her obvious target.

"Mara," he breathed.

"Aye, Ramsay?" She lifted her head just before her lips found him, and he caught the gleam of wicked light in her eyes.

"By God, woman!"

"You promised I could taste you."

"And so you did. I recall—I most surely do recall…"

"You did no' say I could taste you but *once*."

How could he hope to reason with her, while the warm cavern of her mouth enfolded him? "Aye, well," he succumbed, "far be it from me to interfere wi' your wishes."

She made an avid sound, half greed and half appreciation, just before she began to caress him with her tongue. Diarmad promptly forgot who he was, where he lay, and that he had ever possessed any objective other than this. He might happily die in the next moment, so long as he had the attentions of Mara MacIvor first.

And how had she come by such a clever tongue? Not just clever—that did not do it justice. But coaxing, seducing…

Loving.

But nay, that could not be. What they did here, they did for the sake of pleasure and the passion that existed between them. Wracking, unimaginable passion.

The heat of her mouth and the fervent abrasions of her tongue brought him to the brink almost immediately. He reached down to cradle her head between his palms and tried to draw her up.

"Nay, lass. 'Tis enough."

"It is no' enough." The very sound of her voice, husky with her arousal, made his cock jerk uncontrollably.

Desperate, he told her, "But I will come there, inside your lovely mouth."

"Aye, and I will take whatever you want to give me, Diarmad Ramsay."

The power of her passion, combined with his, lifted and further enflamed him. He wanted, och, aye, he wanted. And when she closed her mouth on him again he succumbed to the desire, buried his hands in her hair, and bucked his hips into her, setting up a driven, unstoppable rhythm. She met him eagerly, her tongue a blaze of welcome, and he climaxed in a wave of heat that took the last of his sanity.

Surely he could die now, melted in bliss. But nay, for Mara came crawling up his body, her breasts stroking him all the way, and licked her lips.

"Just as braw as before. Want to taste?"

As he had last night, before he took her for the first time, she pressed her mouth to his. Wicked lass. Och, such a wicked, wonderful lass.

****

"We maun move on away from here," Diarmad said, pulling hard on the strings of what common sense remained to him. "We dare not linger long."

He looked down at the naked woman who sprawled at his feet. Devoid of modesty, she reached her arms above her head and stretched, which caused her breasts to peak enticingly.

"But 'tis still dark," she pointed out.

So it was—if just barely—and he could yet feel the sensation of her mouth on him. How would he ever banish that from his mind?

Did he want to?

"Aye, but the sun will be up very soon, and we need cover to be awa'."

"Aye so." She scrambled to her feet; utterly helpless, he watched. Her hair tumbled down her back like the mane of a pony as she turned and gathered her clothing; her smooth bottom made a potent temptation.

Diarmad fought hard to keep his mind on the matter at hand. "I ha' been trying to figure out just where we are. Can you tell?"

She paused with her garments in her arms and turned her head to look at him. "I have a fair idea. We got turned round after we were captured, but I figure we must be some distance south of Lairg."

That fitted with Diarmad's reckoning. "I do no' doubt you are right."

"We are also in a bit of a predicament as befits the task before us. We are meant to lay a trail and lead the hounds away from the Prince, yet how can we do that now? I do no' think we dare."

"Nay," Diarmad agreed grimly. "'Tis made the more complicated by the fact that we do no' ken what has happened to your adored Charles Edward. Has he been caught? If so, our task has been rendered pointless. If not and he is awa' to France—well, we likewise risk ourselves for naught."

Mara stiffened with indignation. "He is no' my

'adored' Charles Edward."

"Are you certain?" Diarmad did not know why he pressed the matter, save that a terrible thought had just that moment filtered into his mind. Had Mara MacIvor loved him so thoroughly and so well merely because she pretended he was the Prince? Would she treat Charles Edward the same if she could?

The very notion prodded him like a spear to the gut. He scowled at Mara. "Never mind that now. Hurry, lass, and let us be awa'."

They moved off into the gloom of the morning as soon as Mara had gathered their few belongings, all the harmony achieved during last night's intimacies flown. First they bickered over which direction to take; Mara insisted they head due north as they had originally been bidden. Diarmad, who thought northwest a better course, at last tired of the argument and gave Mara her way for the moment. After that, they rode in near silence.

Last night's rain lingered, turned soft as mist. It sparkled on the manes of the horses and on Mara's hair. Riding behind her, Diarmad could not help but admire the warm color of her wild locks as the day strengthened around them. At last the rain clouds lifted, and they found themselves all at once atop a rise.

A great sweep of light arced over the land below. Diarmad drew his horse up, and Mara followed suit.

Ah, and his heart clenched at the sheer beauty of it: wild hills just beginning to green with new bracken and the long bowl of a loch glittering like the water-jewels on Mara MacIvor's hair. The land cradled the water as a mother might her child, and the sky over-reaching all made a soft blanket, moving as the sky so often did in such weather in two directions—one flying east and the other west, with the pure light between.

Diarmad narrowed his eyes against the sudden brightness and felt his spirit take flight with those clouds.

He had undertaken this task for the sake of his father's honor—out of love, aye, for William Ramsay. Now another sort of love touched him, that of place, deeply rooted and as eternal as the rock.

Would he be willing to die for this bonny place? Och, aye.

"It is so beautiful," Mara breathed, and he felt kinship with her flare, oversetting their disharmony. Turning his eyes to her, he saw that with her undisciplined hair and stormy eyes she was just as bonny as this place.

Did she hold him as deeply?

"Aye," he whispered.

"I almost forgot why we are doing all this: for the Prince, aye, but for this most of all." Mara tossed a look at him. "We maun fight in any way we can."

Diarmad nodded as like-minded devotion flared between them. How could this strong and ancient place be held under English rule? That and naught else made the reason so many had died at Culloden.

Mara smiled suddenly. "And I think I know where we be."

He lifted his brows.

"I believe that is Loch Morie. And, awa' over there, Loch Glass. My father brought me here once. If I am right, there should be a wee clachan on the north shore of Loch Morie where we can beg some provisions and perhaps seek word of the Prince."

"What of our pursuers?" Diarmad glanced behind and saw only the height from which they had just descended, all rock and scree without so much as a trail. "Do you think they will track us into the village?"

Mara shrugged, and her eyes met his. "I think we have no choice but to take the chance. And those who come after us must give up eventually."

Diarmad did not see either Archibald or MacNeal surrendering his anger easily, but he did not say so.

"Lead on, then," he said. Given a woman like Mara MacIvor, a man sometimes just had to let her have her head.

Chapter Eighteen

"Wait here," Mara bade Ramsay, eyeing the cluster of cottages at the end of the loch. "Let me ride in alone."

She fully expected another protest. Diarmad Ramsay had an annoying habit of thwarting her at every turn. Had he forgotten she had been sent as his guide? Aye, he tended to do so.

Except last night. They had shared most equally in what passed between them. All at once memory swamped her, complete with taste and sensation. Och, what a body the man had! And how swiftly the taste of him went to her head. Having had him, how was she to keep from wanting him again?

Determinedly, she banished that thought. She must concentrate on the matters at hand, which included keeping him safe—if she wanted to lie with him once more.

And she did—och, she did.

She shot a burning look at him where he sat his pony, his hair gleaming in the morning sun and his eyes holding the look of reserve she'd learned to expect from him. A man of conflicting impulses was Diarmad Ramsay; he wore that skepticism like a second coat, yet get him on his back with a woman's mouth on him, and he flared brighter than fire.

By all the merciful powers, how was she to think

about anything else? She might well ride down into danger, there below—or to her death.

Aye, well, and if she did, at least she could comfort herself with the knowledge she'd had Diarmad Ramsay first.

"Do not follow me down," she insisted, "until I sign."

He nodded. Resolutely, Mara turned her gaze from him and rode down the slope.

The clachan, no more than a group of four cottages, lay quiet. When Mara drew near enough, she saw a few hens pecked about the yards and smoke filtered up from the chimneys. If she did not err in her estimation of their location, this would be MacKenzie country. Would there be any men left, or just widows?

"Good morn!" she called in Gaelic as she rode down, and found her question answered as a man emerged from the nearest shieling. Tall and no doubt once strong of limb, he now bent to the weight of age. A snowy cap of hair topped his head, and he came leaning on a staff. But the eyes that regarded Mara looked quick and perceptive.

"Good morning, mistress," he returned.

"What town is this?" she asked.

"Dunraer. You are on MacKenzie land. Alone are ye, lass?"

Mara ignored the query to pose another of her own. "Any soldiers about?" The way he answered that question should tell her something about his loyalties.

He tossed his head disdainfully. "No Sassenachs here—no' yet."

Indeed, she reflected; the English must not have come, for the buildings still stood whole.

"Have you heard what happened at Culloden?" she asked next.

"Aye, we hear more than you might suppose, even tucked away here."

A woman appeared in the doorway of the cottage behind the old man, and another in that of the next cottage over.

Mara made sure to lift her voice so all might hear. "I would buy some breakfast, if you have any to spare—for myself and another."

"Where? I see no other," returned the old man.

"I dare no' say, but he is an important person and vital to our Cause."

The woman exclaimed softly; she and the elder conferred in rapid words, and then the woman called, "Your esteemed guest is most welcome to all we possess!"

That was the spirit, Mara thought. But could she trust the situation? Cautiously, she asked, "Where are your men?"

The woman pushed past the old fellow. "They ha' no' come back from the battle. Faith, I hoped you might be my husband come now. But others ha' passed through, bringing news."

Mara felt a weight on her heart; she knew this woman's husband likely lay dead.

"If your companion be who we think," the woman called, "go and tell him my house is his."

"Thank you, mistress. I will bring him."

Trust, Mara thought as she turned her mount and rode back up the hill. Dared she? The place appeared peaceful enough and its occupants sincere, but so had that other clachan back when Diarmad saved her from a terrible fate at the hands of those Sassenach soldiers. Death could lie within these cottages, and she worried not so much for herself but for Ramsay.

Somewhere during the night just past, Diarmad's life had become more precious to her than her own.

Ramsay, still sitting his horse, met her with an inquiring blue-gray stare. "Well?"

"I think 'tis safe, and they already suspect your identity."

He grumbled. "I wish I did not have this role to play."

"But you have. Come along; perhaps we can learn something useful."

What appeared to be all the occupants of the clachan awaited them below, standing out in the light. Mara hoped Diarmad's slight loss of luster, his scruffy beard, and stolen boots would not spoil the illusion. His fine coat now bore a layer of dirt, and his hair, no less than hers, hung tangled.

But she had to admit, as they negotiated the slope side by side, he had the bearing of a true prince, head held high, expression composed. Ramsay played his role better than he knew.

And apparently he still appeared sufficiently impressive, for as they approached every head bowed. One or two of the women dropped into rough curtsies, and the old man lowered himself to one knee.

Ah, and Ramsay would not like that. But when she stole a look at him, he remained impassive.

"Welcome!" the old man quavered. "I am Alasdair MacKenzie. All we have, sire, is yours."

Emotion clenched at Mara's heart. Glancing again at Ramsay, she saw some of his stoicism chip away.

How would he handle this?

He swung down from his horse and, bearing still regal, went to the old man.

"Arise, Alasdair MacKenzie. You have no call to kneel to me."

"I ha' every call, liege, if you be who I suppose."

Ramsay met Alasdair's fervent gaze. "No need, even so. You and your companions pay me all necessary homage with the loyalty in your hearts. Do we not all fight for this Cause together?"

Using his stick, Alasdair pushed to his feet. His gaze searched Ramsay's face. "We heard you were on the run, Your Highness, and wi' naught but a lass to guide ye. I hope you will rest here wi' us a wee while. This is my son's wife, Rona. My son went off to yon battle, and I wished right well I was not too old to go wi' him!"

Emotions chased one another across Ramsay's face. For a moment Mara wondered if they would prohibit speech. But he said, "I am honored indeed by your fierce, loyal heart. We would be grateful for any news you have. But we are pursued and would not bring harm down upon you and yours."

"Na, na," Alasdair responded, "do no' fash yourself over that, my liege." He turned to a lad standing nearby, who looked no more than ten. "Geordie, run up the brae and keep watch. Whistle if you see anyone come."

The lad nodded and ran off, back up the way Mara and Ramsay had approached. Alasdair made a sweeping gesture of welcome toward the cottage.

"My Prince, come ye in!"

****

Alasdair and his son's wife, Rona, left their cottage door open to the bright day. But so many people gathered there to peer in they nearly blocked the light. The interior of the cottage—small and humble—revealed clear signs of want, which made what its occupants had to relate even more incredible.

"Thirty thousand pound," Alasdair announced in his quavering voice. "That is the price the English have put on your bonny head, my liege. Can ye imagine it?"

Diarmad scarcely could, any more than back in the cave when MacNeal had brought word of the bounty offered for Charles Edward. Who could conceive of so much money? And how could folk, especially folk in such straits as these, resist that prize, especially when their loyalty had already cost them so dear in the lives of their husbands and sons?

"But do ye no' bother yoursel'," Alasdair immediately assured him. "None here shall betray you. We would no' dream on it, would we, Rona?"

"Nay, indeed." Rona edged closer and offered Diarmad a plate of oatcakes, likely all she had in the house. He hesitated to deprive her of her small store, then thought about her pride in later telling how she had served her Prince the product of her own hands.

"Thank you, mistress."

She blushed. Seeing the pure worship in her eyes, Diarmad had to look away.

"Pray tell me what other news you have," he bade Alasdair.

"We ha' seen waves o' men that survived yon battle pass through—none o' our own yet. They bring word from others they ha' met. That is how we learned of the price on your royal head. But"—Alasdair's rheumy eyes widened—"'tis said you are everywhere! In the east heading for Dunbar, in the west hopping among the islands."

"Well, I am here now. My guide thought to circle around to the north and perhaps shake the hounds from our tails."

"A wise course, if you ask me, my Prince! There is an old cattle trail that leads from the north. I could show ye how to pick it up when you are ready to leave us."

"But do no' go yet," Rona beseeched.

"Aye so," Alasdair agreed heartily. "Our roof is yours for as long as ye wish."

Diarmad thought about what had happened the last time they paused in such a place as this and shook his head.

"Honored as I may be by your hospitality, your safety means more to me than my own. I cannot linger here and endanger you and yours. When those who follow us arrive, you must say you have not seen us." He looked to the door where the others stood listening. "Do you all promise me, most solemnly?"

They nodded, their eyes like stars. Diarmad felt a rush of mingled love and sadness. Surely Highland hearts proved too loyal for their own good.

"We should indeed move on, my liege," Mara whispered.

Rona murmured in protest, but Alasdair got to his feet at once. "You may rely upon our silence!"

"Thank you." Again Diarmad swept the avid faces with his gaze. "Thank you all. Master MacKenzie, will you show us this trail before we go?"

"I will, if you can bear with me, sire. I am no' so spry as I used to be."

Diarmad arose also and turned to Rona. Gallantly, he clasped her hand. "I am humbled to my heart, mistress, by your kind welcome. And I trust your husband will come home safe to you soon."

Even as he spoke the words he knew them to be futile. He could see like knowledge in Rona MacKenzie's eyes, yet she held her head proudly and said, "It makes it all better, my liege, for having met ye."

Was that true? Could it be? Diarmad thought of what the sum of thirty thousand pounds sterling might mean to these folks and quailed at such sacrifice.

"Scotland will never go down to defeat," he declared, "so long as it contains such stout hearts as yours."

Old Alasdair lit with joy. "Come, sire, and let me show you the way to safety."

Back outside, the beautiful day enfolded them. Diarmad could see the lad, Geordie, silhouetted on the height and raised an arm to him in salute. The lad returned the gesture.

Would Geordie also store this memory as a precious thing and someday tell his bairns about the time he stood guard for his Prince? And if so, did it truly matter that Diarmad was not the real Charles Stuart? The memory would be just as valid, as was the matchless spirit of these people.

"Thank you all," he said in parting, "and may God bless."

He and Mara, leading their mounts, followed old Alasdair around the end of the loch and up the opposite height, a trip made ponderous and difficult by the old man's gait. Indeed, Alasdair's breathing became labored before he paused and showed them the beginnings of two paths.

"There is the cattle trail, my liege. 'Tis a good route north and south. Cattle traders—and thieves—ha' been using it for time out of mind. The other path goes on up over the hills and makes a difficult way indeed. I used to take it trapping and hunting when I was a young man. Both lead north, but the weather will catch you on the heights, when it comes."

"Thank you, Master MacKenzie. I would have you turn your back on us now so you will not have to lie if soldiers come after us, asking."

The old man's face contorted with emotion. "No matter, my liege. I would give my life gladly to spare yours."

Humility hit Diarmad so hard he could not speak. Had the true Charles Edward—wherever he was—experienced this? Diarmad only hoped so.

"It has been an honor!" Alasdair declared.

And Diarmad returned, "Nay, for the honor has been all mine."

He and Mara took the path to the heights, knowing the old man stood stiff with dignity and watched them out of sight.

Chapter Nineteen

"So, Charles Edward still lives." Mara spoke the words speculatively as she and Diarmad moved slowly across the hillside. "You ken what that means, Ramsay."

Diarmad did. Had they gleaned word of the Prince's capture or death, they might have been able to give up this mad ruse. He could have gone home.

To what, though? To the absence of his father, and possibly Cainnech, as well. Ah, but if that were so, Diarmad would be doubly needed to take up the place of Chief. And perhaps provide comfort to Una—eventually, when her grief lessened, take her to wife?

Once that would have been his fondest wish; now it lay all tangled up with loss and pain. How could he even consider being with Una if it required the loss of his brother?

And what of this woman here beside him? He turned his eyes toward Mara, which did not afford him much benefit. For here on the path up over the heights the weather proved as Alasdair had warned: what had been sunny below had evolved, as they rode, into a sea of mist and clinging damp that cut their visibility and rate of travel drastically.

Mara appeared no more than a ghostly form on horseback, with jewels of mist caught in her wild hair. Funny how, even so, just looking at her raised his desire.

Night must come, and what then? Hours spent wrapped in her arms, the heat of her mouth upon him, her body welcoming his? Could he hope for any of that? Had last night been just a single, mad episode, never to repeat?

He could not ask her. He would not, for all his desire. But his flesh began to ache, and he had to clench his lips together to keep the question in.

Will you love me tonight? Might I spend myself in you and in so doing regain my strength all over again?

"You did well playing your part back there," Mara went on, apparently taking his silence for concurrence. "But thirty thousand pounds! Can you imagine?"

"Nay," he muttered unhappily.

"Still, I suppose the capture of the Prince would effectively end most of King George's immediate problems. I wonder where Charles Edward is now, and with whom?"

Does she wish she were with him? Diarmad wondered. Does she regret she was not deemed fit to guide the true Prince, rather than a mere substitute? The question that had occurred to him this morning once more raised its ugly head: Had Mara MacIvor loved him so well merely because she fantasized about loving Charles Edward?

If so, it would be both a blow to Diarmad's pride and a sorrow. For he wanted her to desire him. *Only him.*

Such thoughts followed him like the trailing mist. By late afternoon, the fog had turned into a soft rain and gloom hugged the shoulder of the mountain across which they traveled.

Diarmad felt rather than saw Mara shoot him a look. "We should find a place to camp before dark. A fall up here could be fatal."

"Aye." And would they lie together when they paused? Diarmad could not seem to banish the question no matter how he tried.

Mara, now riding in the lead, began casting around for a likely stopping place. By the time she found a small dell half choked with rowan trees, the rain had increased to a steady downpour.

"Here," she bade Diarmad. "You tend the ponies, and I will rig one of the rugs between the branches. 'Twill not be completely dry, but better than naught."

Diarmad drew the horses into the shelter of the copse where they could graze on the soft grass beneath, tethered them, and dragged his and Mara's belongings farther in to where she crouched beneath the rug.

"No hope of a fire, I fear," she said regretfully.

"I do not mind." Diarmad could barely see her face in the dim light, but the very lines of her body called to him. He wanted to retrace the contours with his hands as he had before and taste her all over again.

"Why do you no' take off that wet clothing?" he suggested huskily.

She tipped her head, and her wild mop of hair slid over one shoulder.

"And," he continued, "I will do the same."

She got to her feet and stood facing him. He wished he could read her expression better.

"Ah," she said, "so that is the way of it. Will you expect what you had last night, to have it every night while we travel together?"

"No' expect." He admitted, "Hope. That is…" He

caught back the words he had almost spoken. Here and now he did not care if she wanted the Prince rather than him. He would slake his thirst for her on any terms she offered. He concluded, "If you are willing."

She did not move or speak. He stepped closer, raised a hand to her cheek and caressed it very gently. "Will you accept me, Mara MacIvor?"

Her cheek felt warm against his fingers, her hair damp against the back of his hand. His desire heightened impossibly, yet she still did not speak.

What to do? Cajoling was not easy for him; begging seemed undignified. But he would beg her if he must.

"Well, now," she spoke at last, the words barely a breath, "I ha' been thinking about that all the day long."

"As have I."

"I am not certain 'twould be wise, sharing your bed again."

"Why?" He stepped still closer. "Did we no' suit?"

"Aye, that we did."

"Did I no' please you in my attentions?"

"Och, aye. But that was the fulfillment of a promise and, I think, a reaction to the danger we had faced together."

"We are still in danger." He bent his head so his lips hovered above hers, and her breath hitched. "Terrible danger."

"Aye, but there is another danger twice as strong."

"What is that?"

"I might grow altogether too attached to you. And 'twould never do. I ha' been thinking about that all day, as well. Surely before long we shall part—perhaps to face the hangman's noose or the block, perhaps when this wild chase ends and you go home. Either way…"

Aye so, Diarmad thought. Her caution did her justice. Yet his flesh cried out in protest.

He released her cheek and slid his hands down her shoulders until he captured her elbows. "Wise lass. But the night will be damp and cold. I would do you a service by keeping you warm."

She stiffened between his hands but made no reply. He bent his head and ran his lips along her soft cheek.

"Surely," he murmured between kisses, "'tis not good for you to linger in those wet clothes. Let me wrap you in my plaid, just for the night."

"Just for the night?" she repeated a bit wildly. "And what of tomorrow night? And the next?"

"We will consider them when they come." He planted a kiss at the corner of her mouth and nearly lost his control, a man drowning in desire.

She groaned. "A ruinous course."

"Is it? Would you rather lie alone and shiver until dawn?"

Slowly he reached up and untied the laces on her bodice; she did not protest as he fought the damp strings, his fingers clumsy with eagerness.

"Just tell me 'nay' if you would."

As the fabric fell open, he kissed her throat and her collarbone, slid his mouth downward. When he reached the swell of one breast, she seized him by the hair and halted the progression.

"Nay."

"Nay?" Devastation hit Diarmad, twice as powerful as his desire. Would she truly deny him?

But breathless and hurried she said, "Let us first shed all these damp garments."

****

Mara, weak and absolutely drunk with pleasure, opened her eyes into soft, damp darkness. Her languid sense of security told her she lay wrapped close in Diarmad Ramsay's arms.

The man had promised to keep her warm and had done a braw job of it. His mouth had heated her skin most generously, his hands—to which her flesh could not help but respond—had been everywhere, spreading flame. Now she hovered between feeling shockingly sated and wanting him again.

Did he sleep? After the last time he loved her, he had come to rest with his head beside hers and her body cradled against him, as if he would shield her from the hard ground. His hair brushed her cheek and his breath, deep and regular, trickled across her breasts.

He slept.

Mara smiled. Aye, but she had only to touch him in turn—run the palm of her hand down his hard chest, over his taut, muscled stomach, and wrap her fingers around what lay below—to have him once more. Heady knowledge it was, that made her feel both powerful and helpless.

For she might hold his arousal in her hand, but he held her heart.

She contemplated this fact with a mingling of acknowledgement and sorrow. It would not be a good idea for her to arouse and accept him again. For each time she touched him her feelings for him deepened; each time he entered her she found it more impossible to imagine living without him.

But who could fail to love such a man? One who, clever and courageous, nevertheless made love with such tenderness it touched a woman's soul?

Mara knew herself for lost. She would have done better to cut the connections after tasting him only once, for now the craving rode her very blood. Aye, and even the thought of it made her lips tingle with desire. Powerless to resist, she softly pressed them to his.

He responded groggily, his lips—warm and supple—molded to hers before parting them. His tongue entered her mouth as if he owned it. *He did.*

Could he guess how he now commanded her life? That she would do anything, grant him any request—anywhere they might be—if it pleased him, that she would follow him to the end of the earth if he but crooked a finger?

She'd best not tell him that!

But she would open both her mouth and her legs to him, snuggle down farther beneath his body so the most wondrous part of him, down below, might rest just where she wanted it, between her thighs.

Slide into me, she begged in her mind, unwilling to release his mouth and ask. Surely her flesh called to his without words. No question but he stood ready for the task.

He broke the kiss, and she nearly wept in protest.

"Mara," he said.

"Ramsay, please."

He laughed, and the sound rippled through her like the tremors when they came together. "What is it you want?"

She growled in frustration and tugged his hair with both hands. A suggestive movement of her hips and buttocks invited him in.

"Ah, but"—his voice both teased and caressed

her—"are you no' the woman who doubted she should lie wi' me?"

"I still doubt the wisdom of it."

"Then I would do naught to displease you."

"You do not displease me!" She growled again and pulled his hair harder. He slid further into place, very nearly where she needed him.

"Beast," she breathed.

"Vixen," he returned, with the laughter spilling from his voice. *Dhé*, that laughter could well prove her undoing.

"Do your duty, man!"

"First I must taste you." He slid his mouth down to her breast. Aye, it did seem to be one of his favorite locations on her body. She nearly convulsed with pleasure, but he did not stop there. Instead he kept his mouth moving down, and down.

She gasped wildly when the heat of his mouth met the place where she ached so intensely for him. Och, wonderful man, talented man! If only she could lie with him so forever. So that was what he meant by *tasting*.

Just before the top of her head flew off, she growled yet again, flipped Ramsay onto his back, and straddled him. She stared down into his eyes, now just visible as the morning grew around them.

Aye, dawn approached swiftly, their miraculous night nearly done. Best to make the most of it.

Ramsay smiled at her. "I confess, you do no' look like a woman plagued by doubt."

"Hang that. Prepare yoursel', Ramsay." She lowered herself upon him, and in a wild rush they greeted the new day.

Chapter Twenty

"Tell me about your home."

The request came at Diarmad out of the darkness. Three days—and nights—had passed, and they still traveled a difficult and tortuous course over the hills. The journey took its toll on both them and their mounts, but somehow, when they paused to camp, they had always ample strength for loving.

This night they lay out under the open sky beneath a raft of stars. Diarmad had just finished satisfying Mara full well, and the taste of her still lingered on his lips.

Funny that she should ask about his home, for he had been thinking about just that place and wondering if he might not steer a course there since they already traveled northward. His thoughts and Mara's seemed to mesh uncannily and with ease, of late—just like their bodies.

He ran his hand up the soft skin of Mara's belly and captured one breast for the sheer pleasure of it before he answered.

"What do you wish to know?"

She returned his caress, one hand dancing upon his chest. Mara seemed to have left her doubts about the wisdom of them coupling well behind her and now touched him as if she owned him.

He wondered if she did. Pertinent parts of him—

quite possibly. He had never imagined responding so to any woman.

"Tell me what it was like for you growing up there."

"Ah, a boring tale, that, and surely of little interest to you."

"I am interested." She leaned up and kissed him. "In more than just this princely body of yours."

Princely. Diarmad's own doubts—those he'd managed to banish over the past few days—roared back at him. Did Mara MacIvor want him, or did she still fantasize about Charles Edward? Wondering about that consumed him for several moments.

But aye, perhaps speaking about his youth would make her see him as *him*.

"Aye, well," he began softly, his eyes on the stars, "'twas a good enough childhood save for the fact that my mother passed when I had but seven years."

"Do you remember her?"

"I do, and I remember how my da changed after we lost her. He remained gentle and loving wi' us, but some of the laughter we used to know went away."

"If you do no' mind me asking, how did she die?"

"A fall while out riding the hills. 'Twas not the injuries that took her but the chill that set in on her lungs while she lay." Diarmad narrowed his eyes. "I think my da always blamed himself because he did not go with her that day or find her as soon as he might."

Mara said nothing and, mindful of the fact that she had recently lost her own mother, Diarmad caressed her shoulders and drew her closer.

"But he proved a good father, as I say, and did all he could to make her loss up to us."

"He never married again?"

"Nay, never. There was a woman of our clan, a widow, wi' whom I believe he took comfort for his physical needs. At the time, innocent as I was, I supposed them just friends."

"Ah, I wonder that they did not wed."

Diarmad said simply, "She was no' my mother. You should ha' seen my parents together—no other woman could match her, for him."

Mara tensed in Diarmad's arms, and he felt her emotions spike. Why?

After a moment she asked, "Are you Ramsays one-woman men, then?"

Diarmad had once supposed so; all this while he'd believed for him it would be Una or no one. Oh, he'd had women in the past, but like his father with Meg, that had been a thing only of the flesh. He had never considered wedding any of them.

Now, lying beneath the night sky, he wondered what life would be like if he married Mara MacIvor. To him, she felt as limitless as those stars overhead, but quite possibly her loyalties lay elsewhere.

"I suppose so," he confirmed.

She withdrew her hand from his chest. "Tell me about Cainnech."

"Ah, Cainnech." Diarmad smiled. "He is everything a son and older brother should be. Almost five years separate us, and it seemed my whole life I followed him in everything. Learning to ride, wielding a sword."

And desiring Una? For the first time ever, Diarmad wondered about that.

"What is he like?"

"Good, a good man. Always patient wi' me—far more so than I would ha' been if I had a young lad forever on my heels. And a fine teacher—I learned nearly all I know from him, with some from my da."

"He taught you well at arms. I ha' rarely seen a man fight as you do."

"I am not a patch on him." Diarmad drew breath. "That is why I believe he must ha' survived that battle. He will be home when I get there, I am thinking—strong and hale and already in Da's place."

"Tell me about Una."

For the first time, Diarmad balked. He stirred and tried to peer into Mara's face, half turned from him. "What would you know about her?"

"Have you lain with her as you now lie wi' me?"

"To be sure, no!" He might have thought about it—and about little else—dreamed of the length of her legs and the softness of her breasts. But nothing more than dreaming. "She belongs to Cainnech."

Mara's voice insinuated itself into the night. "Did you no' want to?"

As if answering his own thoughts, he admitted, "A man could no' look at Una and fail to think of her in that way."

"Is she so very beautiful, then?"

"Aye."

Mara fell abruptly silent. Again Diarmad sensed her thoughts moving, but he failed to identify them.

At last she said, "She—Una—holds your heart."

Did she? Or did she only hold his imagination? "It does no' matter," he murmured, half to himself.

"You say she is betrothed to Cainnech?"

"Aye. They meant to wed this autumn."

146

"If I were she," Mara said slowly, "and the man I loved came home to me from such a battle, I would not wait for autumn. I would have him now, wed and done."

Diarmad wondered if Una might feel the same. A woman of mystery was Una, the opposite of this woman in his arms. Mara MacIvor usually made her feelings—and her desires—evident. Una hid hers always. Diarmad still could not say for certain which of them she truly wanted—him or Cainnech.

Cainnech, no doubt. How could it be otherwise? What sane woman would not prefer Cainnech to him?

Yet, if Cainnech never came home…

"What if your brother who is betrothed to her does no'—well, does no' return home?" Again Mara echoed Diarmad's thoughts uncannily. "If you take the place of Chief, will she then expect you to wed her?"

Would she? Diarmad's mind reeled at the thought. The unattainable Una, his bride. Una shedding her clothing for him, her beautiful body naked beneath his.

"I do no' ken." His mind elsewhere, he did not fully notice how Mara once more stiffened against him. "Why would she accept me whilst grieving for him?"

Mara sat up abruptly and glared at him. "I ha' never met your brother. From your description, 'tis clear he is a man of inestimable worth, but has it never occurred to you this Una might prefer you?"

Only in his dreams, when he lay alone in the dark of night thinking on the unlikely and the impossible.

"'Tis kind of you to champion me, but you are right. You ha' never yet made acquaintance with Cainnech. If you had, you would understand."

"Champion you! Is that what you think I am

about—encouraging you to go home and claim Una?"

Diarmad answered honestly, "I very rarely know what you are about, Mara MacIvor."

Her expression, which he could see only dimly by starlight, altered. "Except?" she prompted.

"Except?"

She returned her hand to his cheek and slid it downward in a manner that needed no interpretation. He immediately sprang to life.

"Ah," he said.

"I am here," she told him fiercely. "The beautiful Una is not. Do you close your eyes, Diarmad Ramsay, and pretend I am her?"

He struggled for breath before he returned the challenge. "Do you?"

"Eh?" She appeared baffled.

"When we lie together, when I enter you or when you taste my seed, do you imagine I am *him*?"

"Whom?"

"The Prince—the accursed Charles Edward."

She gasped. "Is that what you ha' been thinking all this time? 'Tis absurd!"

"No more absurd than you supposing I want Una when I am with you." Mara MacIvor wooed him so ferociously, consumed him so completely, he had no thought to spare for anyone else.

"Hmm," she granted before she leaned down and peered into his eyes. "A convincing declaration, but I am not sure I believe it."

She still had her fingers wrapped around the standing length of him, which made it difficult indeed for Diarmad to think clearly.

"Believe it," he growled. "Or, better yet, let me

take you again, and see do I lie."

"You—take me?" She reared back, but did not let go of him. "Why should I not take *you*, instead?"

Pure Mara MacIvor, that, Diarmad thought—and one of the things about her that so delighted him.

"You," she ordered, "will just lie back and endure it like a man."

Diarmad did.

Chapter Twenty-One

"I do not like the look of the place," Mara grumbled as she peered down upon the town below. She and Ramsay lay side by side on their bellies in the bracken, their ponies some distance behind them.

The town, a small fishing port she guessed might be Ullapool, told her they had veered too far west. She must have lost her way at some point during the last five days' travel which, she admitted ruefully, was what came of being distracted by a man she could no longer resist.

Indeed, when she thought back over the past days of their flight, only a certain few moments stood out in her mind: the scare they'd had after coming down from the mountain and nearly riding into a troop of King's men; the constant bursts of rain; the warmth of Ramsay's arms at night, and the way it felt when he ran the palm of his hand up her thigh; the many places where they had made love, including caves, copses, and on one abandoned afternoon the top of a mountain. She barely recalled the course they had set or how she had led him.

Which meant she had failed in her task. For her da and Laird Elliot had entrusted her with this man's safety, expected her to guide him, not couple with him until both she and he became senseless.

Ramsay's fault, entirely, she reflected now. She

had only to look at the man, measure the breadth of his shoulders with her gaze, remember the touch of his fingers, or look into his eyes to want him all over again. The taste of him haunted her, prompted a hunger she could not seem to satisfy.

She glanced at him now before turning her gaze away sternly. He rested his chin on his fisted hands, and the weak sun burnished his hair with streaks of red gold.

"It looks peaceful enough," he offered.

It did, yet a frisson of warning chased its way up Mara's backbone. The town, a cluster of streets and cottages, faced a wide, shallow harbor where boats bobbed at anchor. More small boats could be seen arrayed out on the silver water, with the dots of islands beyond.

"There might be an inn," Ramsay offered. "We could buy some ale."

The longing in his voice reminded Mara of how he sounded at other times, and made her want to knock him back into the bracken and have her way with him.

"We dare not risk it," she told him, and felt him slant a look at her.

"What *do* we dare, Mara MacIvor? Where is this wild chase meant to lead us, and how will it end?"

"I do no' ken."

"But were you no' the one instructed by the fine Laird Elliot, he with all the grand ideas?"

"Aye, though we did no' speak about the end of the chase." Mara frowned. To be sure, Laird Elliot's intentions now seemed unco' vague. Her enthusiasm had carried her beyond any lack, at the time.

When she made no reply, Ramsay pressed his case.

"Why not venture down there as anywhere? Surely if I shed my Prince's garb we could go below and purchase a pint or two like any ordinary couple. We shall say we are newlyweds on a wedding journey."

He leaned in to nuzzle her neck, and her blood leaped within her. Aye, so, and they had been behaving like newlyweds, right enough: all over each other at any given moment.

She drew away—not far. "If you shed your Prince's garb, you shall be stone naked." Ah, and that did not make a safe path for her thoughts. She had now seen Diarmad Ramsay naked many a time, and hoped for many more.

"If I shed the damned coat and wear my old plaid, I should pass muster."

"Wear the Ramsay plaid over a Stuart kilt?"

He grunted and gazed below again. "It does not look busy enough for a town occupied by soldiers."

It did not, yet from their vantage point they could not see the whole street, which curved away from them, and Mara's uneasiness persisted. "What worries me is, since we have strayed so far west, the true Prince may already have been here, and not long since. Should a second Prince appear or even someone taken for him, 'twould mean exposure for sure."

"Ah."

"I am sorry, Ramsay, but a pint of ale is just no' worth the risk."

He glared at her in protest. By way of comfort, she leaned in and planted a kiss on his mouth. Her lips lingered and her blood instantly warmed.

"Is there not something else you would have, rather than a draught?" she asked when the kiss ended.

"Come to think on it, there is."

"I promise it shall be yours—as soon as nightfall," she whispered.

"Not before?"

"Perhaps before." Quite possibly she could not endure until nightfall.

"Compensation, eh?" He lifted an eyebrow. "And just what form shall this compensation take?"

"Whatever form you like." Did he not guess that he commanded her even as the Prince might not? Whatever Ramsay may think, she would never consent to do the things with Charles Edward that they had done together. For she loved it when Ramsay took command of her flesh almost as much as when she rode him like a pony.

"What if I would like an ale first and then you, Mara MacIvor? If there is an inn, we might take a room. Share a whole night in a bed."

"And I might enjoy a bath." The prospect danced before Mara's mind's eye the way flowing ale no doubt lured him. Was it safe? Could she disguise him as an ordinary traveler?

"Come." She slid back from the rise and scrambled to her feet. "Let us see what can be done with you."

****

The inn called Horns of the Moon appeared nearly deserted at this time of the afternoon. Situated at the intersection of the main road and another stony track, it seemed humble and far less well visited than the larger inn Mara could glimpse still farther down the street. Yet uneasiness still shimmied up her spine and made her skin itch.

The prospect of a bath, though, continued to entice

153

her. Her vision of it had now evolved into one wherein she and Ramsay shared the water together, with beguiling consequences.

As soon as they stepped into the inn yard, a lad ran out to take their horses.

"Have we coin enough?" Ramsay whispered even as he surrendered his mount.

She glanced at him. Devoid of his fine coat and bonnet, and with his own plaid covering most of what lay beneath, he looked remarkably convincing as an ordinary traveler. She had combed and bound his hair and bidden him to look like a besotted bridegroom. Surely no one would connect him with Charles Stuart.

"Aye," she returned; the horses they'd stolen from Archibald had proved generously supplied. To the lad she said, "Feed them well and brush them down. They have had a rough journey."

He nodded and led the beasts off, which left Mara feeling even more vulnerable.

She looped her arm through Ramsay's and started for the inn door. "Remember to look smitten with me."

"Will this do?" He shot her a look hot enough to sear her skin and added lightly, "I am smitten with you, Mara MacIvor."

Mara's heart stuttered within her chest. He did not mean it; he merely teased her once again.

"Mara Ramsay now," she returned. "Do no' mistake and call me the wrong name."

"Aye—my wife." He drew her closer to his body, where she could feel its heat. She knew all the contours of that body now, where she only need touch him with her lips to render him hers.

Hers.

And what if she were his wife in truth? Impossible to imagine, but no more than she desired. A vision of the future wavered before her eyes: the two of them inseparable through the years, with a home together, and bairns. She could have wept for it.

She stumbled, and his strong arm caught her up.

He whispered, "Come along, Mistress Ramsay."

They stepped through the main door into the gloom of a large room, nearly empty. The small windows that faced the street bore a century of soot, which dimmed the sunlight; a fire burned sluggishly in the hearth at the far end. A number of tables stood about, all but one unoccupied. A woman swept the floor industriously; Mara wondered how she could hope to see the litter.

She glanced up when they appeared and set her broom aside. "Good day. Did ye want a room?"

The two men sitting at the table looked up when she spoke. Both wore dark clothing and showed no glimpse of tartan—not soldiers, yet Mara mistrusted their appearance. The uneasiness that dogged her intensified.

She prodded Ramsay in the ribs with her elbow. As the male half of a wedded couple it was his place to speak.

"Aye, mistress," he said in the humble tones to which she had bidden him. "If you might ha' one available."

The landlady, a head shorter than Mara and twice as wide, gave them an assessing look, no doubt wondering if they could pay.

Mara leaned toward her confidingly. "We are on our wedding journey, mistress, and would ha' a fine place to…well…" She strove to blush, though the effect in the dim room was probably lost.

The landlady's eyes widened with comprehension, but she said, "A wedding journey now, wi' all the unrest about?"

"We were…constrained and could not wait." Mara laid her hands across her belly in an age-old gesture, and Ramsay stared.

The landlady grunted. "What is the world coming to, just? But you are in luck; I've three rooms upstairs and only one taken."

The two men seated at the table must be lodgers then. Mara had hoped they might soon depart.

As befitted his role of bridegroom, Ramsay asked, "How much, mistress, for a room, a good meal, and some ale?"

"And a bath," Mara put in. "I would give much for a hot bath."

The landlady's brows rose as if scandalized, but she said grudgingly, "We have a room in back where the bath might be set up. 'Twill cost a bit extra, mind, with all that water to tote."

Mara thought of the money in the pouch on the horse she had appropriated—left by MacNeal, no doubt. She nodded at Ramsay, who said, "A pint first."

"The bath first," Mara objected.

"Nay—the pint."

The landlady grunted again, with what sounded like amusement this time, and relaxed a bit.

"Typical newlyweds, are you no'?" She looked at Ramsay. "You will have your hands full wi' this one."

"Aye," Ramsay agreed. "Do I not know it?"

Chapter Twenty-Two

Diarmad stepped into the small room, the air redolent with the scents of soap, bathwater, and woman—Mara MacIvor, to be precise—which seemed to have a powerful effect on him. The last two strong pints he had consumed already rode his blood; the bath had taken some time to prepare, and he had passed the intervening time enjoying the landlord's good ale. It might not be the best he had ever tasted, but it had to be damn close.

The two men conversing in the main room of the inn had left while he supped his ale, giving him close looks in passing. After Mara disappeared into the back with the landlady, Diarmad continued to linger, but not for long. Thoughts of what might be happening in back spoke far too potently to him. He imagined Mara MacIvor submerged up to her luscious breasts in a tub of water and eventually wondered why he should not be there also.

The landlord—a fellow large as his wife was small, with a craggy face and a fierce expression—glowered at him as he went.

"My wife is back there," Diarmad explained a bit thickly. "Newlyweds."

An unexpected grin spread across the landlord's face. "Go ye on," he bade Diarmad, "through yon door there. And enjoy it while ye can. The flames do no' burn so bright the whole marriage on, ye ken."

Aye, so, well, they roared now with searing intensity, Diarmad thought as he let himself into the tiny place and feasted his eyes on the sight before them.

He had to smile. By now he had seen Mara MacIvor in many moods: angry, impatient, frightened, determined, impassioned…indeed, a certain bliss came to her features when he plunged inside her. But naught to rival this. She looked like a woman transported to heaven.

She lounged with her head against the raised back of the tub, hair and limbs floating, her breasts—as he had pictured—teased by the surface of the water. Indeed, he could see her nipples like two tender buds awaiting the attentions of his mouth.

She opened her eyes and looked at him in surprise. He wondered if she would order him out, resent his intrusion on her few moments of peace. Instead a small smile came to her lips.

"I was just wishing for you."

"Were you?" Diarmad's pulse leaped, mirrored by a movement further down. He let his gaze caress her from her toes all the way up.

"Och, aye. Do you think there is room in here for two?"

Diarmad did not. She occupied the full of the tub with her sweet, white limbs. But he felt willing to try.

"Take off your clothes," she bade, "and we will see."

Ordinarily he would resent taking orders from her; in this case, his fingers moved in total obedience. His garments hit the floor as he moved forward, and he reached the tub naked.

"Step in," she invited.

"'Twill be a tight fit."

She gave him a wicked smile. "Tight is good."

So it was. Caught in a haze equal parts ale and arousal, Diarmad stepped into the water—still warm. Mara made room for him, and he slid under her until her white buttocks came to rest on his thighs, with him facing her.

"Ah," he groaned, sure he would come instantly.

She gave him another look. "Let me wash you, husband."

She took up the soap and a scrap of cloth the landlady must have provided. That wicked smile still dancing about her lips, she began washing his chest, his throat, his arms, even as his manhood strained upright in the water.

"Alas, Master Ramsay," she crooned, her voice as soft and caressing as her touch, "you are in sore need of a good scrubbing—everywhere."

"As are you." His immersion in the tub had raised the level of the water well above her breasts. He reached out and cupped one in each hand and let his thumbs caress her as they would.

"Master Ramsay, you are surely distracting me from my work."

"Work, is it?"

"A consuming task, entirely." She leaned forward and kissed him, a searing movement of tongue on tongue. At once she released him and pushed his head under the water, which forced his body further beneath hers; he came up with his manhood cradled between her thighs.

"Mara," he said then, hoarsely.

"Nay, I am no' finished."

She began to soap his hair even as he prodded, searching, between her legs. If only she would part them and straddle his hips, he would be able to ease in.

He palmed her breasts and she caught her breath; her fingers fell away from his hair.

"You have a beautiful body, Mara MacIvor. In truth, you are a beauty withal."

Her eyes widened. "Me?"

"You." He dove forward and captured her mouth. Could she not tell how bonny he found her? Could she not feel the truth?

He lifted her body in the water and settled her where he wanted her. She wrapped her legs around his waist and her arms about his neck, their mouths fused.

No words necessary, then. He began to move in a slow rhythm, and she kept pace, the warm water lapping around them and threatening to spill over. Desire rose in a wild bubble to Diarmad's head and exploded when he came inside her.

She clung to him, her body shuddering with pleasure, her face pressed into his neck.

"Ramsay."

What did it mean, her whispering his name that way, like a word of a magic spell, like claiming? Tenderness for her assailed him, and he cradled her close, raining small kisses on her cheek.

She lifted her face, and they gazed into one another's eyes, still joined below and her legs wrapped around him. Her lips moved as if she would speak, and some powerful emotion brimmed in her eyes, but no words came.

"What is it?" he murmured.

She shook her head, and for an instant a new emotion flickered in her eyes. Fear? Regret?

"I cannot seem to stop wanting you."

"'Tis not a bad thing, that," he told her. Or was it? Aye, the pleasure went easy with them now, but what of later, when they were forced to part?

Very gently, he withdrew from her and set her back in the water. "Perhaps we should try to control our urges."

"Do you suppose we could?" She tipped her head and regarded him; her long, red hair trailed across her breasts and into the water, making him ache to touch. "I did make the attempt before, to no good effect."

Manfully, he proposed, "We might resolve to try harder."

"Aye. Seems a waste, though, when we are still together."

"'Tis up to you, Mara," he told her seriously. "I would do naught to trouble you, not now or later."

She said nothing, and he stirred his limbs. "The water grows cold; I will leave you to finish."

He scrambled to his feet, which brought his manhood into close proximity with her lips. An immediate test of resolve, he thought wryly, and ordered himself not to think about it.

Yet before he could step from the tub, she reached out and cupped him. His startled gaze flew to her; the wicked smile had returned to her eyes.

She leaned forward and tasted him with her tongue, rendering him instantly aflame.

"And where do you think you are going? Ah, no, Master Ramsay; we are no' done."

****

The soberly clad men were back at their table in the corner of the inn's main room, and two companions had joined them. Mara strove to ignore how uneasy their presence made her and to concentrate on the pleasures at hand: a fine dinner of roast mutton and mashed turnips in front of her and Diarmad Ramsay across the table.

Both looked appealing—the hot meal because she had not enjoyed one such in many days, and Ramsay because she had. If she were for some reason required to forego one for the other, she would abandon the mutton and have him up the stairs so fast it would make his head spin.

The thought made her smile in satisfaction. She'd had his head spinning right enough in the bath earlier, when he stood before her—an unimagined pleasure. But it begged the question: what was the matter with her that she could not get enough of this man?

True, he cleaned up very well and looked so handsome in the leaping lamplight of the inn's parlor it took her breath away. But she needed to keep her mind on the matter at hand—playing a part that would serve her country and her Prince.

She supposed, all in all, she should be ashamed of herself. True, in the past she had sometimes contemplated doing the things she now did with Ramsay—what lass did not? But it had been in a hazy, distant way that did not equate with truths such as the weight of him in her mouth when he stood in that water before her. She flushed hot just thinking of it.

He leaned across the table toward her. "Do not look over there, but yon men keep watching us. Who do you suppose they are?"

Mara flicked a glance that way. If she had to guess, she would deem them agents of the English Crown. But why would they be here?

Save looking for the Prince.

Another shiver traveled down her spine, this one not caused by pleasure.

Just then the landlady came to their table, bent on refilling their cups of ale.

In a low voice, Mara asked, "Those men over there, mistress—who might they be?"

"They do no' say," the landlady returned, her tone as guarded as Mara's, "but I think they are hunters. Word came some days ago, you ken, that the Prince has been seen in the vicinity. They near missed him at Portree and followed a trail here."

"Och!" Mara's throat closed with dismay; she dared not look at Ramsay.

The landlady lowered her voice still further and leaned in. "I do no' like giving them a berth, but they will burn the place down if we do no'. And there be a crowd of others just like them staying at the White Rose, up the road."

Ill news, that. Nervously, Mara asked, "And has the Prince truly been seen hereabouts?"

"Who knows? They may be chasing ghosts. Or they may take him. I wish them all in hell."

"Aye," Ramsay agreed softly, and the landlady's gaze focused on him.

Mara said, "We heard there is a braw price on the Prince's head."

"Whisht! Do not speak of it." The landlady immediately broke her own ban by adding, "The sum of thirty thousand pound, 'tis whispered."

"A great and terrible sum," Ramsay murmured.

"Aye, but," the landlady avowed, "no one here will betray him, even for that."

"Men are greedy," Ramsay put in.

"Not when it comes to the loyalty in their hearts."

Mara thought of Archibald and MacNeal and shook her head.

The landlady laid a hand over hers, which rested on the table. "A poor time for a wedding journey, lass. If ye do no' wish to stay here the night, we will understand."

Mara looked at Ramsay. It might be as well to flee while they had the chance. But the prospect of a whole night spent with him in a bed spoke to her far too seductively.

Ramsay shook his head slightly. What did he mean to convey?

"We will think on it," Mara told the landlady.

"You do that. Best not to take any chances"—the woman bent closer—"in your condition."

She hurried off then, and Mara questioned Ramsay with her gaze. He shrugged in answer.

"'Tis your decision, lass. You are the guide."

"Aye, then finish your dinner and let us hie upstairs."

Chapter Twenty-Three

Darkness soft as velvet filled the chamber and cradled Diarmad just like the featherbed he and Mara MacIvor shared. After days spent sleeping on the rocky backbones of hill and glen, the humble room seemed a welcome haven. Indeed, he had scarcely imagined such comfort.

And he might never again—at least not soon. He knew very well they should be away out of this town full of king's men and back over the hills. He meant to tell Mara MacIvor so, as soon as they finished loving.

If they finished before dawn. He had already taken her once in a hot flurry, raw with desire. To his shock and disbelief, he still wanted more.

She lay for the moment with her head on his shoulder and one hand splayed across his chest. Sated as he should be by the wild ride just past, he longed to feel her mouth upon him even as it had been earlier, in the water.

A man could happily die after such treatment. He would not mind losing his life so.

Below stairs, guests still lingered and sound rose into their chamber like the echoes from another life. Diarmad heard the rumble of voices punctuated by the shrill tones of the landlady. Someone clearly in his cups began to sing and another voice joined in.

None of that could touch Diarmad here, it seemed.

He inhabited a magical pocket of existence exclusive to him and this woman, full of darkness and fire.

"Mara," he whispered, "will you have me again?"

"You know I will and gladly."

Their naked bodies rubbed and meshed as she crawled atop him. He felt the brush of her hair across his shoulder, followed by that of her tongue at the corner of his mouth.

Had ever a woman been so willing, so generous with her favors? Ah, but she must be able to read his mind, guess just where he wanted that mouth of hers…

For now it hovered above his lips, her clever tongue suing access which he promptly provided. She dove into him, and he nearly gasped with pleasure. Not loathe to play the aggressor, his Mara—and he did not mind a bit.

When the kiss became so intense he could not tell where her mouth left off and his began, he seized her hair and gently urged her on down.

She laughed. "Ah, so that is the way of it!"

She planted a hot, open-mouthed kiss at his throat before beginning to move downward. Her body slid over his as it descended, leaving him aching with need. She kissed the trail of hair that led like an arrow down his belly and paused, making him groan.

"Do no' play wi' me, woman."

She laughed again. "But I like playing, Diarmad Ramsay, especially with you. What will you give me if I do as you require?"

Anything. But he could not admit that. He caught his breath. "What do you want?"

She trapped him between her hands and he nearly came off the bed. She clucked her tongue which, in his opinion, made a terrible waste of that supple instrument.

"Nay, now—'tis not fair if I have to ask. I would hear what you offer."

"For the love of heaven—"

"Nay, better for the love of this great instrument here."

"I will return the favor, whenever you wish."

"Tempting! I do love the feel of your mouth on me. Do you?"

"Do I what?"

"Enjoy the feel of your mouth on me."

Aye, so he did—some places more than others. Between her thighs, she tasted like honey wine. He grunted assent.

"Then that seems no sacrifice."

"Sacrifice, is it?" Diarmad strained his mind. He had naught to offer this woman she'd not already had.

"State your price," he said desperately.

"I will not ask one too high."

"Naught could be too high," he avowed.

"Your devotion? Your name?"

That froze Diarmad where he lay, struck as with a blade of cold iron. What was this? For what did she ask—his name? As in…marriage?

"Ah, now, Mara—" he began raggedly, "you canno' be serious."

"Serious as death," she assured him. "Has the prospect not crossed your mind?"

It had, aye, but only in a hazy, dreamlike way. This whole journey seemed like some mad dream, something apart from his true existence. Ever since his father perished in the bloody squalor of that shieling, he had walked an unknown path that encompassed danger, its only constant the two of them, he and Mara MacIvor, together like this and bonding ever more closely. He could no more see the end of the relationship than the end of the chase.

He caught her face between his hands. "But," he protested, "this is no' serious as death, is it? We are just providing each other comfort and pleasure for a time."

Even as he spoke the words, his mind thrashed wildly beneath a rush of regret. The last thing he wanted was to hurt this woman.

"So." He could not readily identify the emotion in her voice when she spoke. "You do not foresee an ending for us?"

"I foresee my ending, as we have said, on the block."

"And this—what we do together—is just pleasure."

"Is it no'?" *Searing, near-inconceivable pleasure for which a man might well trade his soul.*

But his name?

Once more he tried to imagine it: himself taking this wild lass home to the north, installing her among his folk. Installing her as Chieftainess, if the worst happened and Cainnech failed to come home.

"Mara," he said, "you would no' wish me to make such an offer were I to deem it a 'sacrifice.' "

"Has it no' occurred to you that I—" She broke off abruptly as they both became aware of a commotion on the landing outside their door: raised voices, what sounded like protests, and the tramp of many boots.

Mara had no time to leap up from her position before the door of their room flew open. Light flooded in.

"Nay, you shall not!" The landlady stood with her back to them and her arms outstretched, barring the way into the room to those beyond.

Aye, those beyond—Diarmad had an eyeful of a small crowd of men in black clothing and identified them instantly. His heart leaped into his throat.

"What is this?" Mara hissed.

Diarmad knew all too well: capture. Their incaution—his incaution—had led to this and trapped them now like rats in a basket.

"Out of the way, mistress!" one of the men cried. "This is king's business."

Mara, still crouched naked above Diarmad's chest, stiffened in horror. He cradled her with careful hands, shifted, and thrust her behind him in the bed.

Where had he left his sword? On the floor with his shed clothing. He reached out and groped for it even as the landlady set up a spirited defense.

"This is a safe house, and you will no' disturb any guests of mine. These folk are a young couple on their honeymoon."

"That man is Charles Edward Stuart—the Pretender himself," one of the intruders replied. "And you, woman, will hang for abetting him."

Diarmad swore, heartfelt, even as his searching fingers closed around the hilt of his sword.

"Charles Edward?" the landlady echoed. "It is never. Tell them, Hamish."

She appealed to her husband, who apparently lingered back in the crowd, under guard or no, Diarmad could not tell.

The king's man did not give the landlord a chance to reply. "We were given word that the Pretender was here in Ullapool. That is he, beyond there, with his strumpet." He said to his comrades, "Take them."

Irony of ironies, Diarmad thought bitterly even as he slid from the bed and took up a fighting stance, naked as he stood. The one moment he did not play at being the accursed Prince, he was taken for him. And this would surely prove a death sentence for him. If he could free Mara, however, he would.

She huddled now at the far side of the bed, uncharacteristically silent. He hoped she would do nothing foolish and so get herself hurt.

"You shall not!" the landlady cried again. "That lass is wi' child!"

"Is she?" The leader of the troop stepped forward where Diarmad could see him clearly. Tall and rail thin, clad all in black, he looked like doom on two legs.

Peering into the room, he said, "I am Arthur Dwight, agent of his majesty the king, and I do arrest you in the king's name."

The landlady spat, "That great English toad is no king of mine."

Dwight struck her without hesitation, knocking her off her feet, which started a scuffle behind—the landlord no doubt striving to defend his wife.

Mara cried out in dismay but, trapped on the other side of the bed, could not reach the woman.

Grim but steady, Diarmad raised his sword.

Chapter Twenty-Four

Mara gasped as the first clang of steel on steel assailed her ears. Ramsay's sword leaped forward eagerly to meet that of his opponent, and she hauled herself up by the edge of the bed with no thought for her nakedness. Her eyes marked the limited space and the spot where the landlady had fallen. She tried to count the men at the door but could not see them all.

She knew—none better—how Diarmad Ramsay could fight. But she did not suppose he would battle his way out of this.

They thought him the Prince—the true Charles Edward. Terror soured Mara's stomach. She had always known it might come to this. But now, when it came, it befell the man she loved.

Aye, and she had just been going to confess her feelings for him when this horror erupted. How many times had the words hovered on her lips these past days? Every time he loved her, which had been often enough.

Upon the thought, her questing fingers found what they sought on the floor: the handle of the dirk she'd found on her mount after they left the cave.

Diarmad Ramsay might well go down, but he would not fight alone.

The sound of ringing steel now filled the chamber. Mara surged to her feet with the dirk in her hand and saw that Diarmad looked to best his opponent. What a sight he made fighting naked as born. But, though the doorway of the room made a bottleneck, an untold number of king's men waited beyond.

Well, she could but hope to narrow the odds.

With a wild cry, she launched herself at Dwight, who stood to one side, the only other man in the room. She did not care for modesty—did not even heed her nakedness—and came at the man with her dirk flashing.

He went down beneath her assault, and the landlady screamed. Mara, feeling the man's body beneath her, struck blindly, bent on doing as much damage as possible. Dwight grunted but did not strike back; he had hit his head on the wall as he fell.

Mara scrambled back to her feet, blade now wet with blood, and snarled, "Who is next?"

The bottleneck at the doorway burst and men flooded in.

Things became wild and desperate after that. Mara later remembered slashing at whomever she could reach, before hard hands seized her naked flesh. Her awareness spiked in one terrible moment when Ramsay, rushed and overwhelmed, became pinned to the wall. His sword clattered to the floor, and Mara found herself slammed to the bed.

The room went abruptly silent save for a great deal of ragged breathing, some of it Mara's own.

She turned her eyes to Ramsay but could barely see him for the number of bodies hemming him in.

Dwight, who had already struggled to his feet, stood with his hand pressed to one shoulder.

"As I began to say: Charles Edward Stuart, you are under arrest for treason against your king." He glared at

Mara, who lay winded, sprawled on the bed. "And is this your Highland trollop?"

No reply from Diarmad. Mara's pounding heart leaped painfully. Was he dead? Mortally wounded?

Dwight snatched a sword from one of his men and pointed it at Mara's naked breast. "Is what the landlady says true? Do you carry his brat?"

Quite possibly. Lately the idea had hovered in Mara's thoughts that she might cradle not the Prince's but Ramsay's bairn—beloved, cherished child.

"Speak," Dwight ordered and pressed the tip of the blade to her flesh.

"Do not harm her!" The landlady arose. "What kind of monster may you be that would slay a lass wi' child?"

"My good woman, this particular child might prove quite dangerous." Dwight lowered his blade to Mara's belly. "Best to spay her now and make certain."

"Nay!" A struggle erupted over against the wall where the men hedged Diarmad. He emerged from among them with fists flailing and his desperate gaze reached for Mara. "Harm a hair of her head," he spat at Dwight, "and I swear, on my honor, you will die for it."

Dwight drew himself up. "And, sir, what 'honor' is that? The same that would usurp the throne of our rightful king?"

"I am no' Charles Edward Stuart!" Ramsay bellowed. "My name is Diarmad Ramsay, and she is my wife."

"I suppose," Dwight drawled, poking with the point of his sword at some object on the floor that Mara could not see, "that is why you wear the royal Stuart tartan."

Mara, the blade withdrawn from her belly, breathed again. But Dwight soon swung the sharp point back toward her.

"Get yourself dressed, harlot. You men, subdue our guest. We will take them both."

The landlord and his lady began to protest; Mara barely heard. Her gaze met Ramsay's across the intervening distance, and she saw the emotion that filled his eyes.

Despair.

****

They were hauled under heavy guard from the Horn of the Moon Inn and down the road to the White Rose, where Dwight had his headquarters. Ramsay had also been ordered to dress while Mara, already clad, stood in Dwight's grip with the point of his sword at her throat.

"Make no mistake, sir," he told Ramsay. "One wrong move on your part, and I will bleed her even as she has bled me."

At the White Rose they were taken into a large room filled with guards, where Dwight immediately searched their belongings, finding Ramsay's fancy coat and bonnet.

"Not the Pretender, eh?" he challenged then.

Ramsay lifted his chin. "Nay—just a newlywed couple on our wedding journey."

"Why deny it, sir?" Dwight turned to face Ramsay, who stood between two guards. Mara, huddled some distance away, could only wish she were at Diarmad's side.

Dwight drew off his own coat and signaled to one of his men, who hurried to him. Dwight had bled through his shirt, and he shot Mara a hard look before he said, still speaking to Ramsay, "The truth will be far too easy to prove once we reach Windsor."

Windsor? Mara had never in her life been so far as Edinburgh. Ah, to be taken from this land she loved, maybe held in a dark cell only to have her head parted from her body—and never see Diarmad Ramsay again.

Her gaze flew back to him where he stood, his mien disdainful, his anguish visible only in his eyes, which did not so much as flick toward her.

"Aye, the truth will be proven," he agreed, "and you made to look the fool."

Dwight's gaze raked Ramsay even as his attendant began to swab the wound at his shoulder, the worst of those Mara had inflicted on him.

"You wish to make a game of it, do you, sir? Very well; there have been numerous sightings of you all along this coast and about the western islands. The loyalty of these rebels is such that, even for a hefty reward, none would betray you—until now." He gave a grim smile, turned his head, and called to one of the men at the door. "Bring the witness."

Ramsay did glance at Mara then, a startled look that betrayed his surprise. She tore her gaze from his to look at the door—only to see Neal MacNeal appear, a grimace on his lips and bright avarice in his eyes.

"Good day to you, Your Highness," he said.

****

Diarmad saw Mara wobble and begin to go down but could not reach her, trapped as he was by two men with swords, one to either side of him. Still, he knew how she felt; MacNeal's appearance affected him like a solid blow to the gut.

Aye, and their goose was cooked now, right enough. No way to talk their way out of it, which had been his one, admittedly dim, hope. They would be hauled away to Windsor at best—slain like dogs at worst. His mind tripped over the likely series of events: even if, upon reaching England, he stood exposed as an imposter, MacNeal's testimony would brand him an ally of the Prince, guilty of treason.

Well, he had known from the first, when he gave his da his promise, it could come to this. At least he'd got the chance to meet Mara MacIvor, with her wild courage, and spend some time in her company. He thought again of how she'd flown at the English king's agent, naked and armed with only a dirk, an inspiring sight. And at least he'd had the chance to lie with her— repeatedly—a thing that would warm him to the block and the waiting grave.

Now he drew a breath and gave MacNeal his coldest glare. "Who is this man? I do not know him."

"Not know me, Your Highness? Did you no', only a while since, offer me my own kingdom?"

"I did not." Diarmad gazed past MacNeal. "Sir, this man no more knows my identity than I do his. He weaves you a story for the sake of the price on Charles Stuart's head."

Dwight and MacNeal both looked startled. Mara MacIvor struggled up from the floor.

"Not true," MacNeal decried. "Sir, our men captured this pair above Loch Morie and sought to hold them for the reward—"

"There you have it," Diarmad put in swiftly.

"He admitted his identity then! And he bargained with me, offered me untold wealth in exchange for his freedom."

"And did you accept that bargain?" Dwight's voice sharpened. "If so, you may yourself stand accused of abetting him and be charged with high treason."

MacNeal's jaw went slack with dismay. "Nay, but it was no' like that. I meant all the while to turn him over to the authorities of the Crown, such as yoursel'!"

Dwight, tight with pain as his man bandaged his shoulder, leaned toward MacNeal slightly.

"Then why did you let him go? Offered you a better deal, did he?" He snapped at the guards, "Hold him, men. Hold them all!"

Chapter Twenty-Five

A doleful situation, and no mistake. Diarmad Ramsay, watching the dawn creep in over the windowsill of his small prison, fought the despair that gripped him. Cold to the bone, he believed this one battle he must lose.

Well, Da, he spoke to his father in his mind, *it has come to this. Whether as the Prince or as his ally, I will meet wi' death. A wide, dark river it seems, from where I stand, though one you ha' crossed before me. Will you be waiting for me after the axe descends?*

The hairs stood up on the back of his neck at the thought, though his father gave no reply. Had Diarmad truly expected one? Scowling, he made a determined account of his scanty arsenal of weapons. He had his wits, and little more. But he and Mara MacIvor still lived, and she made a formidable weapon in any situation—a bit heedless and headlong, perhaps, yet just thinking on her heartened him. He had already determined if but one of them survived this it should be she. He would say and do whatever he must, lie and bend his honor to assure it if he could.

He did not know that he could, but it brought to mind another possible advantage: the doubts which the king's agent, Dwight, clearly harbored about MacNeal. Well, what right-thinking man of any nationality would not doubt that blackguard? Dwight must have some decent instincts to which he might ultimately listen.

And the Prince—the true Prince, presumably—had been sighted in the area. Should he be seen once again while Diarmad and Mara MacIvor remained in Dwight's hands, then that should provide further doubt.

Diarmad frowned still harder while staring at the new morning. Of course, it might not be the true Prince who had been seen. Other teams like his had been sent out as decoys. If he and Mara had gone astray, so might they.

He would gladly sacrifice another set of imposters in order to get Mara free. The capture of a second team might accomplish that—as would the capture of the true Prince.

And when it came to it, Diarmad would sooner sacrifice the safety of that benighted royal than others like himself who merely sought to do their duty at the cost of their own lives.

Aye, and what did that make of his honor? If he bent it now and failed to protect the accursed Charles Edward, did that violate the promise he had made to his father? For his honor might be bent but not broken yet.

His father's spirit did not need to appear before him; Diarmad knew what he would say: *Play the game through to the end. Convince them you are Charles Edward and buy our true Prince more time to get safe away. During your journey to Windsor, aye, and even to the block, he may well get away to France.*

Sacrifice. His father had made that at Culloden. And honor bound as he was, Diarmad should be willing to follow his example.

He was. But cursed if he would take the courageous Mara MacIvor with him.

Nay, if he fought on—if he continued to lie and resist—it would be for her sake, not his own.

****

"Stand there, sir."

Dwight snapped the order from behind his breakfast table where he lounged at apparent ease. Diarmad had been hauled into the dining room by a passel of three guards and stood before him like an errant child.

Still for all that, Dwight's uncertainty made another presence in the room. The man did not know what to make of Diarmad and so must have decided to employ intimidation.

The isolation of the night just past had been intended to further that, as was Dwight's lordly attitude now. Would the true Charles Edward wilt under such circumstances? Hard to tell.

Sick as Diarmad's stomach felt with anger and honest fear, the breakfast spread on the table smelled tempting. The landlady's fine dinner seemed all too long ago.

Act on Mara's behalf, he told himself, and the Prince be hanged.

"Where is my wife?" he demanded.

"Your wife, is it? You mean the trollop who may carry your royal seed?"

"She is my wife, and though many generations of stout Scotsmen stand behind me, there is naught royal in my blood."

"MacNeal says there is."

"MacNeal is obviously a rogue who has his eye fixed on the head price laid on the Prince." Diarmad lifted his head. "He has naught to do wi' me."

Dwight examined him with cold, gray eyes the way a surgeon might probe a wound. "Where were you married?"

"The priest at Runfrel. Send one of your men to ask him, if you will." Or better, do not. Diarmad had never been to Runfrel and did not know if a priest dwelt there or not.

"And why were you wearing the Stuart tartan?"

"Wedding finery is no' so easy to come by these days. Those things were lent to me—which is why the plaid does no' match the kilt."

"And the jacket?" The gray eyes narrowed. "'Tis a fancy garment, that, for a Highland bridegroom."

"Lent also. It pleased my wife, though." Diarmad allowed himself a scowl. "I doubt it does now. I demand to be reunited with her at once."

"You demand? Sounds like a prince, that."

Diarmad drew a breath. "You have no right or cause to keep us apart, and us newly wed."

Dwight tapped his clean-shaven chin with one long finger. "I will admit you looked like newlyweds when we burst in upon you. But there may still be cause for arrest."

"Cause? What cause?"

"Those weapons you and your purported wife carry, for one—it is not permitted."

"Not permitted for Highland men, perhaps. Does the decree include women?"

"It includes all! Besides, she attacked me; I could take her away with us for that, with or without you."

Diarmad's heart fell.

"Best, I think, to take all of you back to Windsor on the strength of my suspicions and let the authorities there sort it out."

"What of our wedding journey?"

Dwight sneered. "The most unlikely aspect of all. Who would take such a journey in this climate?"

Ignoring the listening guards, Diarmad leaned toward the king's agent. "My wife had her heart set on it—a short sail to the islands, which is why we are here. Sir, you ha' met my wife, a woman of some... determination."

"Indeed."

"I did no' like to disappoint her."

"Then, sir, you are a fool."

"Perhaps so, sir." Diarmad fixed his gaze on Dwight's. *Forgive me, Da*, he beseeched inwardly. "But I swear to you, I am not Charles Edward Stuart."

Was that a flash of capitulation in the man's eyes? Diarmad could not tell.

"I will speak again with MacNeal," he said, "and make my decision."

"Aye, but only let me be confined with my wife. 'Tis cruel indeed to keep us apart."

Dwight's lips twisted bitterly. He spoke to one of his men. "Put him in the chamber with the woman, but double the guard. Bring me the other prisoner; this will not take long."

Diarmad's spirits lifted slightly. Surely if Dwight truly suspected him he would not grant such a favor. And just the thought of being with Mara gladdened him.

He followed the guards without word or protest. They had shut Mara into a tiny side room on the ground floor—not so much a chamber as a cupboard. She sprang up when the door opened and Diarmad stepped in.

Only one small window, high up in the wall, admitted any light. It showed him the worried expression in Mara's eyes, as well as unmistakable signs that the indomitable Mara MacIvor had spent at least part of the night in weeping.

No sooner did the door close behind Diarmad than she threw herself into his arms. "Och, by heaven, are you all right?"

She clutched him so fiercely he could barely answer. Unexpected emotion rose to choke him. The hard lump that had rested all night near his heart abruptly melted.

"I am. And you?"

"I scarcely know. I ha' been worried half out o' my mind that they had taken you away, and me shut in here never to see you again."

She drew back just far enough to look into his eyes. Hers were awash with tears. "I ha' never been so frightened."

"Ah, now, Mara, I would no' have you worry for me."

"I can seem to do naught else."

He saw her lips tremble and, driven by impulse, stilled them with his own. Her emotions leaped at him: terror, uncertainty, longing, and something far sharper that mirrored his own feelings. The kiss, intended to comfort, swiftly became far more.

But Diarmad hauled himself up; this made no time for passion, though each time he touched this woman the flames leaped higher.

"List now," he said as she clung to him. "We may no' have much time together. Even now Dwight questions MacNeal and may well speak wi' you next. Mara, lass, you maun deny everything."

Her gaze met his once more, and he wondered what he saw in her eyes. Aye, he knew this woman now, with her fierce, loyal heart. Could he count on her to betray her adored Prince?

"Deny?" she echoed.

"I ha' just come from the man's presence and have him half convinced we are naught more than the newlyweds we claim. You maun say the same, lass. I told him the clothes I carry are wedding finery lent to me, and that we were wed by a priest in Runfrel. You must say the very same, or he will never believe us."

Thoughts chased one another through her hazel eyes. He guessed what words she would say even before she uttered them. "But surely 'twould benefit the Prince more should we let these soldiers haul us off to Windsor."

Diarmad tensed. "It might."

"And surely 'tis what we promised our fathers—yours and mine—we would do. Anything we could, to spare the Prince's life."

"Aye, Mara; my honor lies in chains to the promise I gave my father on his deathbed. And while that may include offering my neck to the axe, I cannot bring mysel' to risk yours." Why should this woman, glowing with life and courage, sacrifice herself for the sake of a man who had withdrawn from the field of battle even while his supporters died?

Diarmad's loyalties had become impossibly twisted. He suspected Mara, far more straightforward, would choose a different course, and he did not know how to persuade her otherwise.

But her eyes once more filled with tears; she reached up and trapped his face between her hands.

"I do no' wish to see you die, Diarmad Ramsay, not in Windsor or any other place. May God—may my da!—forgive me."

He kissed her, unable to resist the sweetness of it. Her lips clung and molded to his and her emotions rushed at him still more intensely, not passion this time but something strong as a pledge.

Stronger than the promises they had made to those they loved?

Diarmad had no time to contemplate the question. From beyond their prison came a sudden commotion, raised voices, and someone calling for Master Dwight.

Mara MacIvor stopped kissing Diarmad and stared into his eyes. "What is that?"

Diarmad shook his head. "I do no' ken, lass, but you'd better begin hoping for a miracle."

Chapter Twenty-Six

Mara stood holding her breath while she watched Diarmad Ramsay scale the wall of their prison. The place, not long ago a cupboard or storeroom, now contained little besides a narrow cot and a slop bucket, but the shelving gave Diarmad enough purchase to climb up and seize the window frame. That being done, he then pulled himself up by his arms in a show of easy strength.

The window, far too small to permit escape, let in only limited light and offered a narrow view of the inn yard. Mara waited while Diarmad surveyed it and descended once more.

He shook his head. "I can see little save soldiers stationed all about the inn. The commotion must be out front."

Mara paced in the cramped space. "What do you suppose has occurred?"

"It could be aught, from the arrival of a messenger to another troop coming in. We shall have to wait and see."

Wait they did. The time drew out, while the light coming through the window shifted and Mara's terror faded into a persistent sickness in her gut that competed strangely with hunger and thirst. No one came near them to offer news or refreshment. At last she sank to the edge of the cot, even her nervous energy worn down.

"Surely," she spoke after an interminable length of time, "if the king's agent meant to drag us off to England, he would have begun the journey by now."

"Aye," Ramsay agreed.

"Waiting is so very hard." To Mara's dismay, tears flooded her eyes. She made a point of seldom weeping foolish tears. And in her opinion she'd already wept enough in Ramsay's presence.

The last time, he'd kissed her tears away. For some reason that memory only made her weep harder now.

"Ah, lass." He came and sat on the cot beside her, his warmth a balm. Before she could think to long for it, he gathered her into his arms and onto his knee.

Mara tucked her head beneath his chin and hung on tight. Was this the last time they would ever hold one another? All at once she could not breathe for fear of it.

"What if they separate us?" she whispered.

His arms clenched her spasmodically before they eased again. "I hope they do."

"Eh?" She tipped her head so she could meet his eyes. "Why?"

His lips twisted in a grim smile. "If they drag me away to the south, I pray they leave you behind. I will do my best to argue for that, if given another chance."

"But nay, we are in this together. Why should you pay the price alone?"

"Because my one comfort, should I face the block, would lie in knowing you still run free wi' all your beautiful, wild courage."

"Beautiful?" Mara repeated, plucking that word from the others. He had said that once before, but did he truly think her so? Her sister, Janet, had always been the bonny one. Mara's flaming hair and freckles demoted her to what folks usually described as "spirited."

"Och, aye," he whispered, and ran his lips along her brow. "If the worst comes, Mara MacIvor, I will carry with me an image of you taking on that king's agent with naught but a dirk in your hand."

Ah, her nakedness: that explained it. But would she quibble? Nay—she would take any compliments that fell from this man's lips, warm, soft, and winsome as those lips were.

She had just drawn breath to press her mouth against his when there came a jingle of keys from outside the door, which almost instantly flew open.

Ramsay leaped to his feet with Mara still clutched in his arms. The breath she had drawn suddenly scorched her throat.

Four guards stood clustered in the hallway outside. The foremost of them spoke. "Come."

Ramsay stiffened. "I will come with you, but pray, leave my wife here."

"Both of you!" The fierce brandishing of a sword accompanied the order. Ramsay set Mara down carefully and caught her hand.

Her heart thudded to her feet as they went, surrounded by guards. The soldiers' grim expressions indicated she walked not to her release.

I was right; that was my last time in his arms. If only I might have had that kiss for comfort.

The main room of the inn, where they had been before, teemed with people and confusion. Mara saw Dwight with a number of his men gathered around him, along with a fellow she took to be the innkeeper and

188

two additional men who stood under close guard.

Her breath caught in her lungs again, painfully, for one of those two looked remarkably like Prince Charles Edward Stuart.

Ramsay's fingers contracted on Mara's so hard it hurt. The soldiers herded them to the table where Dwight stood facing the other captives. They all stared at one another for a moment suspended in time.

And then, slowly, Ramsay sank to one knee. Startled, Mara followed.

****

He must be the Prince, the true Prince. Mara's heart drummed in her chest even as her mind struggled over it. Given, she had seen Charles Edward only once, and that from a distance. But this man looked enough like the remembered face and form to be him, or his twin. And Ramsay had seen him more than once during the battle. If Ramsay knelt to him now, this must be the true Prince, indeed.

"Ah." The word came from Dwight on a note of satisfaction. "So you acknowledge your Pretender!"

"Get up!" Charles Edward cried at almost the same moment. "Fools—I am not the Prince."

Ramsay arose, dragging Mara with him, but kept his head bowed. "Of course you are not, my liege."

Dwight grunted. "Is this not an interesting set of circumstances? I appear to have netted not one prince but two in these fecund western waters."

Mara lifted bemused eyes to the pair, both males, who stood under guard. One wore the rough garb of a clansman in Gordon tartan. The other, quite resplendent, caused her eyes to narrow.

Was he or was he not? At second glance she could

not be certain. Much of his glamour was lent by the clothes he wore—finer even than those given to Ramsay and blazing with the royal Stuart plaid.

His face, quite handsome beneath a head of well-dressed hair, now bore an expression of extreme consternation.

Dwight went on drawling in his hateful southern dialect. "I need only discover which prince I should haul away to Windsor and, undoubtedly, the block."

"I have told you from the first," Diarmad argued, "I am no prince. I am on my—"

"Wedding journey, yes," Dwight finished it for him, "with a bride to boot. Our other royal guest has no such ready story and was apprehended attempting to board a boat some distance south of here. Bound for France, sir? Or just leading us on another merry dance among the islands?"

The Prince pressed his lips together and looked desperate. What, Mara wondered, would the true Prince say in these circumstances? Surely once caught he would own up to his identity and in all honor keep from letting blame fall on those who served him, would he not?

Then again, this might not be the true Prince. Mara had not laid eyes on the other decoys sent off to play their game. If this were one of them, would he not be sworn as were she and Ramsay to protect the Prince at any cost? Her head spun.

Ramsay squeezed her hand. He, clearly, had chosen his course and abandoned his role as Prince. Mara could not quite decide how she felt about that. It bent his honor, aye—yet he did it for her sake.

"I demand you let me and my wife go," he said to

Dwight, "as you now have your quarry."

"You do a lot of demanding," Dwight spat. "There is still the small matter of the arms you bear and the fact that your wife bloodied me."

Ramsay lifted his head. "My wife is a woman of spirit and, er, her passions were enflamed at the time. I am that certain you will no' wish to bother wi' us," he nodded at the other captives, "now that you ha' bigger fish to fry."

"But," the Prince spoke, his honor apparently no brighter than theirs, "I have been telling you all afternoon, I am not the true Prince. There was a scheme—decoys were sent out. For all I know, these two are part of that."

"Eh?" Ramsay stiffened in apparent outrage. Mara realized with some shock that their lives now rested on his talents as an actor. "Would you accuse me of such treason?"

"He accused you and himself," Dwight said thoughtfully, and the Prince bit down on his own tongue. "It seems," Dwight went on, "I am faced with a choice. Drag all of you to Windsor or just the most likely pair."

Chapter Twenty-Seven

Diarmad's heart beat so hard in his chest he could barely think clearly. At his side, Mara MacIvor was for once silent—praise God—and Diarmad cradled her fingers, his touch a warning. He no longer cared much what happened to him so long as Dwight let her go. He knew very well what his father would say: carry on with the deception, lie as he must to protect not Mara MacIvor but Charles Edward.

Diarmad's priorities, though, had changed. He now placed the welfare of this woman at his side above that of anyone else in the world.

What did that mean for him, for his heart? No time to contemplate it now. He merely hoped she could keep from saying something rash and incriminating.

Dwight turned cold, gray eyes on him. "What say you? Are you part of this scheme of which your Pretender speaks?"

Fervently, Diarmad shook his head. *Forgive me, Da.* "I have told you who and what we are: innocent travelers. If you put her through this proposed ordeal, my wife may well lose our child."

"Might just be for the best, that." Yet Dwight appeared still more uncertain. He eyed Mara, no doubt wondering how it would appear should he turn up before his superiors with a distraught, grieving woman.

He turned his gaze to the other pair of captives.

"Pray, sir, tell me more of this scheme to lead us on a series of false trails."

The other Prince exchanged looks with Diarmad. "I am honor bound to speak no more of it."

Swiftly, Diarmad challenged, "Honor, Your Highness, like unto that which saw you flee the field of battle at Culloden when so many stood and died for you?" True anger colored his voice, and it made Dwight lift his brows.

To the supposed Pretender he said, "This man bent his knee to you, sir, but it seems he does not fawn at your feet." Abruptly he jerked his head at Diarmad and Mara. "Let them go."

The soldier to whom he spoke stiffened in surprise. "Sir?"

Dwight, his gaze focused on the second set of captives, drawled, "If there is such a scheme afoot, no one would be mad enough to involve that she-devil in it. What man would choose to lumber himself with the likes of her?"

Relief washed over Diarmad, encased in disbelief. He drew Mara closer to his side, willing her to remain silent just a bit longer. It would be like her to exclaim indignantly and declare herself part of the scheme Dwight decried.

Possibly frozen in surprise, though, she said nothing.

Diarmad nodded at the king's agent. "Thank you."

"I do nothing for you, man. In my opinion you are all rebels in dire need of extermination. But I have no wish to drag that"—again he jerked his head toward Mara—"halfway across Britain. And"—his lip curled—"I would not further interrupt your *wedding trip*."

Still Mara remained miraculously silent. His heart pounding and half expecting to be called back, Diarmad pulled her from the room and no one objected. Not even the other prince, whose eyes met Diarmad's once more just before the door shut behind them.

He spoke but one word to Mara. "Hurry."

They passed the landlord, who had exited the room before them, and found themselves on the street with evening gathering in from the hills. Diarmad sought to orient himself; it seemed a large part of him had been left behind in that place.

Including your honor. Was that his father's voice he heard in his mind? William Ramsay, he knew, would have seen the thing through to the end, never shirked the full of his duty, and never shifted blame to another.

Diarmad had just walked away, leaving those other men—fellow imposters or true Prince and his guide—to face certain death.

What does that make of you, lad?

He flinched inwardly. Aye, that was indeed his father's voice.

"Come," he told Mara and headed off down the street even as he began to argue with his father in his mind.

Had it been but me in danger, Da, I would have stayed and faced my fate. What I did, I did for her sake.

You mean, his da returned, *the woman who herself volunteered for this task and fought like a she-wolf back there?*

Aye.

He peered into Mara's face—bone white with tension. Why did she ask no questions, make no protests? In all the time they had been together, she'd rarely remained silent so long. Was she struck dumb?

He told her, "We must collect our horses and belongings from the Horns of the Moon. Hopefully the landlady will have our things kept safe. And then we must make some distance before that man back there changes his mind."

No reaction, not so much as a nod, though her fingers remained fast in his and her feet kept pace. What thoughts possessed her mind? Did she agree with Diarmad's father and mentally denounce Diarmad for a traitor to her blessed Cause?

But Da, he argued on in his mind, *I paid a dear enough price to that Cause at Culloden—as did you. I will not pay with her life as well.*

Ah, and he would have time to explain it to Mara when they were safe away. But what would her reaction be? Would he lose her regard? Would she now despise him?

The landlady at the Horns of the Moon greeted them with astonishment and called her husband. "Only look, Hamish—our newlyweds ha' been released." She laid her hands on Mara's shoulders. "And are ye all right, lass? Those brutes did nay harm you?"

Mara, still not uttering a word, shook her head. Disquiet twisted Diarmad's gut.

"We maun away and swiftly, mistress," he told the landlady, "before yon Sassenachs change their minds. I thank you for all your kindness."

"Ah, and was I no' young and newly wed once? I can see just how in love the two of you be. Hamish!" she bellowed to her husband. "Have the lad bring their horses, and you fetch their bundles. Wait here," she told Diarmad, and hurried away.

"Mara." He turned to her and battled the distress he saw in her eyes. "This is the right thing to do, as I am sure you will come to understand."

Before she could answer, the landlady returned with a parcel which she pressed into Mara's hands. "Some food for your journey, and God bless."

They met the lad with their horses in the yard. Still with one ear cocked back up the street, Diarmad helped Mara mount and stowed their bundles, which the landlord passed to him.

"Go safely," the landlord bade, and they rode out the way they had come, Diarmad with his shoulder blades twitching.

His father remained silent as they wended their way through the village and northward—as did Mara MacIvor. He set a fast pace, unable to put the town behind him quickly enough.

As they rode, evening fell and the dark settled around them like a protective cloak. When Diarmad could no longer see Mara's grim, set expression, he drew up and caught her bridle.

They had followed the trail northeastward out of Ullapool and now put the sea behind them. A small copse of trees stood to one side; Diarmad dismounted and led the horses there. At last he lifted his arms to her.

"We can rest here the night." Not far enough from their imprisonment for his liking, but surely Mara's silence meant she had been shattered by her experience. Best not to continue stumbling on through the night.

Besides, he needed to hold her, avail himself of the comfort they had shared before. Perhaps her lips and the warmth of her embrace might quiet the voice in his mind.

She slid down from her mount into his arms but moved away immediately. Diarmad felt the rebuff like a breath of cold wind.

He let her unburden her horse and spread their belongings on the ground before he approached her again. By then he could barely see her face for the gloom beneath the trees, but he felt her resistance when he caught her shoulders between his hands.

"List to me, Mara. What happened back there—it had to be done. I might hold my own life ransom to my honor, but not yours. Understand?"

"Leave go of me." She jerked from his grasp and moved away quickly. Wrapped tight in her cloak, she curled into a ball on the ground with her back turned to him.

Diarmad did not approach her again.

Chapter Twenty-Eight

"Mara, we must speak together." Ramsay drew his horse to a halt on a rise.

The ache lodged beneath Mara's ribs intensified. Two days had they ridden—blindly, it seemed—after leaving the benighted town of Ullapool with their skins intact. For Mara the time had passed in a blur, all gratitude mixed up with dismay.

Now she refused to look at the man beside her— could not bear to—and gazed instead at the beautiful scene below. Her throat grew tight with emotion; she had now seen more of this bonny land than she had ever hoped or dreamed, and it proved far grander than her heart could hold.

And this man she loved?

She turned her head at last and feasted her starved eyes on him. The afternoon sun lit his hair with a ruddy sheen and sculpted every line of his proud, handsome face. As rugged, stern, and strong as this land was Diarmad Ramsay—and as beguiling.

Determinedly she turned her gaze away again as shame gripped her. She longed for his touch but in two days had not succumbed to that desire. She listened now as his voice caressed her ears.

"This course is run," he announced. "I am finished wi' it. I do no' ken what you think of the choice I made back there. You will no' say." He left the words hanging as if questing for a reply.

Mara cleared her throat, hoarse from disuse. "Was that the true Prince?" she asked. "Was it our liege lord we left in chains?"

Ramsay did not immediately answer. She stole another look and caught sight of his profile, hard and tense.

"I do no' ken for certain, but I think not."

"You saw the Prince at Culloden."

"I saw him, aye, and that man back there was a very good likeness, very good indeed."

Silence once more fell between them while Mara struggled with the pain in her heart.

Ramsay said, "I know what you are thinking."

Did he? A wonder that, because Mara certainly did not.

Before she could say so, he went on.

"You hate me for breaking my vow to my father, forcing you to break your vow to yours, and for betraying that man at the White Rose, be he prince or no. You ha' lost all regard for me. And you believe we should carry on with this mad chase all about the Highlands, pretending to be who we are not."

Hate him? Was that truly what he supposed? Nay—he did not know what she thought at all.

And how could she tell him? How admit that amid this sea of mangled honor, duty, and obligation her concern was so selfish and personal?

"If you do no' intend to carry on wi' our assignment, what do you intend?"

He gazed at her now with heavy gravity in his eyes. "I mean to go home. I have obligations there. My father is dead. I do no' ken whether my brother still draws breath. But for all that, my clan will need a chief."

So that explained the direction he had been heading, steadily north and east toward what must be his home lands.

Pain clenched at her heart still more fiercely as truth struck. It was over, this mad, beautiful dream. "You wish to be shed of me," she said, not without bitterness.

"Eh?"

Somehow she held his gaze. "I know it must be so."

He shook his head as if bewildered. "It but strikes me I maun offer you the choice to go home also. That has been borne upon me by your silence, if naught else. 'Tis no' fair for me to set off on my own course and not give your feelings due consideration. If you wish, we will turn back and I will tak' you home before going on my way."

A death stroke to Mara's heart! She swayed where she sat. "Part ways, you mean." She had been right, then; since the encounter back in Ullapool, since hearing what Dwight had to say, he saw her differently. She could not bear it, could not part with him despite what he might think of her. But should she beg to accompany him? What of her pride?

"I ken fine you do no' agree with my decision to leave off wi' our task," he said rigidly. "And if you would sooner see the last of me…"

She looked away at the glorious backdrop of hills and sky, unable to bear what she took for loathing in his eyes.

"How near are we to your home lands?"

"A day or two's ride, maybe three."

"Then"—she couched it in a way her self-esteem, battered as it was, would allow—"'twould be far better to continue on there rather than delay by turning back. Your lands seem a fair enough place to go to ground while the search dies down. I can always leave for home later."

And perhaps meanwhile he would decide he could not live without her despite her great and intolerable failings.

He gave a hard nod. "Very well so. We will ride on together."

****

Together, yet not together; Diarmad thought about the truth of that later when he lay beneath a blanket of stars, searching the heavens for answers. The only ones he found, he could not stomach.

Mara lay barely an arm's length away from him, yet far beyond his reach. Their conversation this afternoon proved how she now despised him.

But he ached for her, he did still—longed even now to draw her into his arms, hold her close against his body as he had before, woo her lips and make her his completely. Her desire had been so hot and ready, her favor so strong, losing it felt akin to a mortal wound.

Aye, but he could not blame her for shunning him, could he? He had known from the first moment they met how she worshipped her Prince. And yet he, Diarmad, had forced her to abandon her hero, or one who valiantly served him.

What of your honor, lad? He heard his father's voice in his ear again, harsher than ever in life.

I could no' let her be hauled away to die, he

replied silently. *Surely you maun see that.*

But his father's reply indicated he did not understand. *Cainnech would have done as bidden, would have carried through and kept the Ramsay honor whole.*

At the cost of her life, Da?

At the cost of hers, and his own. Did I no' bleed away my life for this Cause?

Aye, Da.

What of all the others who ha' made a terrible sacrifice? Are there not poor, suffering folk even now who would starve rather than claim the price on our Prince's head?

Archibald and MacNeal—

Would you try to justify your actions by comparing yoursel' with that sort? You truly have condemned your family's honor.

Tears flooded Diarmad's eyes, blurring the stars overhead. *I have shamed you.*

His father did not refute it, and pain lodged like a stone beneath Diarmad's heart. He vowed to the sky, *I will no' fail you again.*

Once more his father made no reply. Diarmad lay with his eyes brimming and tried to imagine his future. If his brother survived and had made his way home, he, Diarmad, would have to do his best to support his new clan Chief and live with his burdens. Might Mara MacIvor fit into that life? Could he do anything to change the dire way she now saw him and persuade her to stay?

For of all the unimaginable things before him, parting from her seemed the most impossible—losing her fire and brightness from his days, watching her ride away to the south knowing he might never see her again.

Nay.

His weighted heart protested it. Yet his aching mind told him, *She already despises you.* Why ever would she agree to stay?

He closed his eyes tightly against the blurry stars and his ears against the terrible voice of condemnation. He could not—would not—regret buying Mara's life at the cost of his honor, but it seemed a terrible price, losing her regard and affection.

Come to me, he begged her silently, but she lay in her blankets with her back to him, and he dared not reach out.

Not for all his longing.

Chapter Twenty-Nine

Home. Diarmad reined his horse involuntarily on the crest of the rise and gazed into the glen below. The sun, sinking low into the west, shed golden light across the well-known scene like a balm of magic, and his battered heart tried to rise. He had been too long away and far too sorely tested, but love of the deepest kind still rooted him here.

Aye, his da might have said, and that love is why men such as we fight, bleed, and die—for love rather than loss, and for belonging most of all.

For once, Diarmad and his da agreed.

He belonged here and wanted never more to stray. Was he willing, though, to live in this place under England's iron heel, as opposed to being free?

He sensed more than saw Mara MacIvor glance at him. He tore his gaze from the beloved scene below and fixed it on her.

She looked weary, worn, and as filthy as he. Her hair made a wild, red tangle around a face still far too pale and drawn. Doubt and darkness yawned in her eyes.

"Rest soon," he assured her, "a hot meal, and something to drink."

She merely nodded, words from her still being few.

He would scarce believe the lass he had met after Culloden could be so silent.

But she cleared her throat and spoke after all. "So that is your home. 'Tis beautiful, just."

"Aye, beautiful." He did not tear his gaze from her face. Still, in an effort to reassure her, he said, "You may regain your strength here before you go off home."

Her face tensed, and the darkness in her eyes flared. "As you will."

"Nay, lass—as you will."

She looked away from him, her profile rigid. "You must be anxious to get home; let us ride on."

****

"Master Diarmad!" The cry split the air in this place that, to Mara, seemed almost impossibly peaceful. After the discord behind them—battle, fear, and death—Ramsay's glen appeared untouched, as if somehow magically removed from the rest of the world.

Could it be real? Mara blinked as they rode down the slope, and peered at the lad who hurried to meet them. Tow-headed, he had not yet achieved the ability to control his thin limbs, and they flew out like bent wings. But his face shone with gladness.

"Eamon," Ramsay returned, his voice happy but his expression guarded.

The lad reached them and stayed Ramsay's horse with a hand to its bridle; Mara drew her weary mount to a halt.

"I am that glad to see you!" the boy exclaimed. "Laird Elliot has been and gone; he brought the terrible news even before our men came, carrying the Chief's body. The rest of us—we kept praying you would return home."

Ramsay looked at the cluster of buildings ahead,

his heart in his eyes. " 'We'?" he repeated. "Lad, tell me my brother, Cainnech, awaits me."

"Nay, master." The lad's mobile face dissolved into tears. "Ne'er say you did not know? Laird Cainnech did no' come home."

Diarmad rode the rest of the distance in grim silence, and Mara followed, her heart aching with all the pain he refused to show. The settlement, nestled beside a quiet loch that shone mirror-like in the last of the light, looked ancient, its stone works far older than the present structures.

Folk came streaming out to meet Ramsay as to a beloved son, relief—and grief—visible in their faces. Before they even reached the main building, which must be the Chief's house, Ramsay and Mara were forced by the press of bodies to pause. Ramsay swung down from his horse and helped Mara down after.

Mara, standing by in silence, learned much from that scene. The affection of these bereaved folk flowed at Diarmad Ramsay like a tide of welcome and claiming. Women, old men, and children made up most those gathered—had the bulk of the young men been lost in the south?—and only a few men of fighting age appeared, all bearing injuries.

He belongs here, Mara thought, as fundamentally as that light slanting in from the west. He will become their light now that his father and brother are gone, whether he likes or not.

He was right to come home, his instincts true. But surely she, Mara, would lose him to these demands.

You never had him, my girl, she told herself sternly. Oh, perhaps she had held his body for a time, while he played at being someone else—kissed his lips and fancied she might touch his heart. But now he saw her for what she was and, anyway, none—*none*—of that had been true.

Indeed, caught fast in greeting his folk, clasping hands and giving assurances that aye, he had returned to stay, he appeared to forget Mara's very existence.

Upon that thought she caught sight of yet another figure hurrying toward them.

The crowd surrounding Diarmad parted for her as for a strong wind, though she moved far more gracefully than any mere rush of air. Indeed, something fluid accompanied her movements, and her long, black hair flowed out behind her as she came.

Mara did not need to wonder who she was—the name supplied itself. Una, she who was supposed to wed Diarmad's brother. She who now pushed through to Diarmad's side and reached with both hands to claim him, sharp gladness visible on her beautiful face.

And he? Mara saw him close his eyes as for an instant of prayer or in gratitude for longing answered, and she felt her heart slowly break into a thousand pieces in her own breast.

****

"Laird Elliot brought us advance word of your father's death, and Seumas here news of Cainnech's loss, when he made it home not long since."

Una spoke the words softly, even her sadness unable to detract from her beautiful, musical voice. Mara, seated among the group gathered near the small fire in the Chief's house, tried not to hate her, and failed.

Their group consisted of Ramsay and herself, Una, the aforementioned Seumas, and an older man called

Gregor—a contemporary of Diarmad's father who, as advisor, had been helping lead the clan during the absence of the Chief and his sons. Seumas, a friend of Diarmad's and, apparently, Cainnech's, had been gravely wounded in the battle and now went on sticks, his handsome face contorted with pain.

Una... Just thinking of the woman lifted Mara's hackles. She sat as near as she could to Diarmad's side, speaking in that soft voice, plying him with food and drink, and touching him whenever she could with her narrow, white hands.

Mara remembered all too well what Diarmad had said of her—she had been betrothed to Cainnech but had never revealed to whom she had given her heart.

Aye, well, she showed it now, right enough, with her every word, every gesture, and each glance from her lovely eyes.

Those eyes—they should be as black as her hair; instead, large, misty gray, and as mysterious as an autumn morning, they dominated her face.

Mara had been introduced to her, to all of them, yet Una's eyes just skipped over her as if the woman considered her insignificant. As evidently she was, to Una's world. And to Diarmad Ramsay's? How could he spare so much as a glance from the woman beside him?

So far he had not. They'd gathered at the Chief's house ostensibly to discuss the clan's situation, but so far their talk all centered on how desperately the clansfolk, and Una, needed him.

The older man, Gregor, watched it all with grave concern. The younger, Seumas, had been one of those few surviving clansmen not present at Chief William's death, and due to his injuries had not had the honor of helping convey the body home, a loss he seemed to feel deeply.

"I arrived too late for his burial," he told Diarmad when they met, "to my sorrow. Your father is up on yon hillside with his ancestors."

Mara had felt it then, the weight of history that settled on Diarmad's shoulders.

And now as he sat with Una's fingers on his forearm and the firelight flickering over his features, Mara acknowledged the fact that aye, she had lost him—lost what she never truly had.

"I learned of Cainnech's death before I left Culloden," Seumas told Diarmad, pain sounding in his voice. "I had the sad task of bringing that knowledge home. I reached here with the heavy news only a few days after your father went into the ground. They told me when I got here that you were off about your mission sworn."

His face dark with grief, Ramsay asked, "I suppose you are certain my brother is dead? There is no cause still for hope?"

"Nay cause for hope—I met up with Callum, who was at Cainnech's side when he died and who died himself soon after I found him. He was fighting alongside Cainnech, the two of them having been cut off from the bulk of us by the push of the battle. He said Cainnech slew many Sassenach soldiers before he fell."

"He is lost to us," Una said, tears filling her eyes, "and not even his body brought home."

"It is a tale of sorrow," Diarmad stated flatly, but his fingers clasped Una's where they lay on his arm.

Una leaned toward him. "You are here now, Diarmad, and your presence gives us the heart we so sorely need. These times are black, aye, but as Chief you will lead us out of them."

"Aye, Laird." Gregor spoke quickly. "As the last member o' your father's house, you are the man to help us begin again. 'Tis what your father would ha' wanted, and your duty is to wed and beget a new generation to lead us. Only that can heal the past."

"I am no' certain aught can heal it," Diarmad objected.

"'Twill no' be easy," Gregor confirmed, "but as always before, you will do as your da would wish."

Aye, Mara thought, her heart aching, and his duty lay in the lovely Una's arms.

Chapter Thirty

Diarmad glanced up and beheld Mara MacIvor approaching across the green sward that fronted the Chief's house, the sun in her hair. As always when he saw her, his heart rose unpreventably before he could discipline it.

Mara MacIvor no longer wanted him, had barely come near him since their arrival here. Aye, plainly she despised him, and he could see by the determination etched on her face that only duty brought her to him now.

Five days he had been home, and the glen and its occupants had welcomed him with warmth that could not be mistaken. Indeed, early summer seemed to touch the hills; even the weather had been soft and kind. The beauties of this place he loved assailed him anew.

If you love it so, why were you reluctant to sacrifice all for it? Once again he heard his father's voice, still sterner than ever in life. *As I did, as Cainnech did.*

I was willing to sacrifice my own life, Diarmad answered yet again, silently, returning his gaze to Mara MacIvor, *but not hers.*

The folk of Clan Ramsay, including Una with her oft-times discerning mind, had chosen to welcome rather than chastise him for that. But Mara MacIvor had been there, and he believed he now saw judgment in her eyes.

Indeed, those eyes met his for only an instant before fleeing to the hills at his back.

"Good morn," she greeted him. "Where are you bound?"

Diarmad gestured wordlessly to the hillside behind him. Each day he had walked to his father's grave, seeking a solace the voice in his head refused to allow.

Cainnech did not and would not lie in this bonny place. As Seumas had related with sorrow, Cainnech had been buried in a mass grave at Culloden. Another sacrifice Diarmad could not hope to repay.

Respectfully, Mara said, "Pay your homage and take your time. I will wait here for you, for we need to speak together."

Diarmad's heart fell. Aye, for days he had known this must come. She meant at last to chastise him, condemn him for his lack of honor. He could see the intent and sorrow in her eyes.

Take it like a man, he bade himself. Yet he found Mara MacIvor's regard meant more to him than he might have dreamed.

He remembered how she had looked at him once—as if he had hung the moon in the sky, as if he were the very Prince she worshipped. He recalled the hazy desire in her eyes when she ran her tongue down his body and took him into her mouth.

No more.

Woodenly, he asked, "Of what do you wish to speak?" As if he did not know. "I can go up the hill later."

But she shook her head.

Impulsively, he invited, "Come with me, then."

The place where William Ramsay lay commanded a breathtaking view over the glen and clear to the mountains beyond. Not so much farther north, as Diarmad well knew, lay the shining sea. As a boy he had climbed up here often, knowing on a clear day he might glimpse a distant strip of darker blue beneath the horizon.

This had been a burial place for Ramsay Chiefs through the ages, ever since the first, who carried both Scottish and Viking blood, had built a roundhouse below.

And would his bones one day lie here also? What would the years between then and now hold for him?

"'Tis easy to see eternity from here," he said to Mara.

"It is a bonny place," she replied, looking at the stones, some crumbling, that marked the graves. Slowly she raised her eyes to him. "It suits you."

"Eh?" He eyed her warily, thinking how beautiful she looked with the morning breeze stirring her bright hair. "You think so?"

"Och, aye—you look like one of the ancients come walking out of the mist of time itself." She smiled ruefully. "You no longer look at all like the Prince."

Aye, so. And did that explain this distance between them? She had only desired him because she could pretend he was Charles Edward—that was true after all. Now she saw him as an ordinary man—nay, less than that, with his tarnished honor—and no fit object for her affection. Curious how that did not make him want her any less. Even now he ached to take her in his arms, press his lips to hers, and experience again her sweet, hot tide.

But he had lost her regard and something most precious from his life. *There is sacrifice for you, Da.*

"Let us speak together as you will," he offered.

She gave him a wry smile. "Should we speak here and risk offending the ancestors?"

"I imagine that depends on what you mean to say."

She turned and sat at the verge of the rise overlooking the glen. Slowly he joined her in the damp furze.

She gazed out over the glen, and he took the opportunity to feast his eyes on her profile, fearing he knew all too well what she would tell him.

But she said, "As I say, you belong here, and your folk need you. You did the right thing putting aside the chase we led."

All the breath left him in a rush. "You think so?"

"Aye, I do."

He fumbled for words. "Then you do no' despise me for breaking my vow to my father?"

She turned her head and searched his face. Her eyes met his at last.

"I was no' certain about it at the time, but now I see what lies here and I understand. You were honor bound to your father, aye—and to your Prince. But a different, stronger, more ancient honor binds you here."

"I am glad you understand." He swallowed hard. "I would no' have you think any less of me."

She tossed her head. "Does it matter? Can it possibly?"

"Aye."

Now, abruptly, she avoided his gaze. "I understand full well the ties between the heart and the land. The old stories tell how our ancestors traipsed through the southlands and across the narrow sea in search of their heart-places. Yours lies here, and many duties pull at you."

"Aye. I wonder if my father would agree."

"He made his choices, Ramsay—and paid for them. Now you must do the same."

"And where, Mara MacIvor, did you acquire such wisdom?"

"Along the trail we trod together, a hard and rocky path." She shot him a glance. "Now it is time for me to leave."

Diarmad's heart fell again, this time like a stone from a precipice. So strong was his dismay, for a moment he could not speak.

She fell silent also, a state that still seemed foreign to her.

At last he said, with a miserable attempt at calm, "So soon? But you ha' barely caught your breath."

"Aye, indeed, it is tempting to linger a while in such a place."

"Then stay. You are most welcome."

She gave a tight smile. "Welcomed by the new Chief, eh? That should count for something." When he started, she went on, "'Tis what you are now, Ramsay—Chief of this place and doubly bound to it. But whereas you belong, I do no'. And there are those who would sooner see me gone."

He searched her face. "Who?"

"Are you so blind? Una, for one."

"Una?"

"Ah, Ramsay—'tis true what they say. A man is a man, for a' that. And it seems often a man does no' see what is in front of him."

215

"Speak plain, Mara MacIvor, if you will. You did no' used to utter riddles but said what you meant."

"Nay, for I am a heedless, shocking creature, am I not?"

He frowned, puzzled. "Eh?"

Her face drew taut, and for an instant he saw agony—and was that shame?—in her eyes. "Remember what you told me soon after we met? That you had feelings for a woman back home, but she was betrothed to your brother, who would be Chief. You said you never could tell where her heart actually lay, for she was a careful woman and full of mystery."

"Aye," Diarmad allowed, his heart sinking further.

"Well, I am here to tell you—as a friend, if I can yet claim that name—you need no longer wonder. Una still means to wed the man who will be Chief, and he is you."

Diarmad stared at the hills which blurred before his eyes. Aye, he had always desired Una—what man would not? But it had been a fine and distant desire, nothing like what he felt for this woman beside him. It contained no intimacy, no memory of touch or scent. Una might well be a goddess, with her skin of cream and that fall of black hair that reached nearly to her knees. But he did not know the intensity of her passion, or the way she would clench around him when he plunged inside her. He had never watched a storm of emotion gather in her eyes.

Mara MacIvor seemed made of emotions, all of them honest and true. The two women, he suddenly saw, could not be more different.

He said, feeling his way in it, "You are mistaken; she has said naught to me of marriage."

"Well, she would no', would she? A woman with her dignity." Mara spoke the last word wryly, though Diarmad did not understand why. "But I see how she looks at you. She will expect you, in time, to ask for her hand."

Diarmad tried to imagine it: approaching Una with such an intention, winning her hand, making her his own. Kissing those lips as he had so often dreamed, taking her to his bed. A future, full of bairns and aging, spent working for this place.

Would there be laughter? Would there be storms of passion and warmth that overcame them? Would there be brightness that pulled at his spirit?

When he failed to speak, Mara said, "I see this is a new idea for you, if a welcome one."

"I suppose in my heart I always thought her Cainnech's, after all." Cainnech always desired the best and won the day.

But…was Una the best?

"Circumstances have changed," Mara said with what almost sounded like sadness. "Go and speak wi' her if you doubt me."

"I do no' doubt you." Never that. Diarmad shot a look at Mara, tried to discern her feelings, and once more failed. He went on, "Much needs deciding here, including plans for the future. That will take time. Moreover, Una has no true say in what happens." Not yet, anyway. "I am trying to tell you, you need not leave so soon, Mara MacIvor. Stay a while yet." Near as he could—would—come to begging.

But she shook her head.

At the urging of his heart, he went on, "It may no' yet be safe for you to travel south. Better to wait until the dust settles, until the Prince is out of the country."

"Or dead?" Her eyes moved to his. "We are still neither of us certain if that man we left in Dwight's hands was he."

"Not certain, nay, but I do believe him another imposter such as myself."

Aye, and they had shared so much, from the terror of Archibald's cave to those perilous moments at the end. How could he let her just ride from his life?

Yet he could not get round the fact that she wanted to leave, and that she went so far as to bid him wed another. Did he need further proof that whatever she may have felt for him had died?

"Mara, stay," he bade her again.

"Go speak with Una—settle your future. Then you and I will talk once more."

Chapter Thirty-One

"I hoped we might speak together."

Diarmad delivered the words from the doorway of the ladies' chamber, a room in the Chief's house where women gathered to do their needlework. Long ago, Diarmad's mother had reigned here, and it had been a place of warmth, laughter, and sometimes silliness. Since her death, clanswomen still gathered, but the chamber had lost most its heart.

Now Una sat here with two companions, she working at her weaving. Most women spun wool or fashioned garments, but Una had always made tapestries depicting scenes from the clan's history.

She looked up now and fixed Diarmad with a somber gaze. But she sounded warm when she answered, "Of course. Did you wish us to speak alone? We can walk out."

But her two companions arose and, with an exchange of smiles, laid their work aside. Diarmad stepped in, and they went past him, out of the chamber.

"Come and sit," Una invited. "It seems we need not walk out after all."

He approached her slowly, unable to keep from admiring how lovely she looked. She had plaited her dark hair into a thick braid that trailed down her slender back, confined about the crown by a thin, silver band that very nearly matched her eyes. The light streaming into the room warmed her flawless complexion and made her blue gown glow like a jewel.

Nay, she could not be less like Mara MacIvor. Impossible to imagine Una riding him in a victorious show of desire or attacking a man with a blade in her hand, naked as God made her.

Una patted the bench beside her. "Of what do you wish to speak?"

And after all, he did not know how to begin. Mara could be mistaken; he might make a fool of himself. He looked instead at the tapestry. "On what are you working?"

"It is a scene depicting the landing of your ancestor, Raold Ramsen. You ken fine I mean to chronicle all the clan's history before I am done. I will, in time, make a cloth showing the battle at Culloden— once the grief becomes bearable."

Diarmad looked into her eyes and wondered about her grief. He saw no stain of sorrow, only the calm composure she usually presented.

"You must be devastated at Cainnech's loss," he said. "After all, you were set to wed in autumn."

"Aye." Her hands stilled on the threads in her frame. "Difficult to imagine him as dead, with that great laugh of his stilled and all his kindness flown. Especially when…when I did no' see his body. I keep expecting him to walk through that door even as he used to do, fresh from practice at arms, with the smell of sunshine in his hair."

She did love him, Diarmad thought. And she missed him even as did Diarmad. He, too, had trouble believing all Cainnech's strength and energy gone from the world. He had followed Cainnech so long. Should he follow him also in marriage to Una?

"Did you wish to speak of Cainnech?" Una asked.

"I would no' grieve you by doing so."

"Nay, but life maun continue on, Diarmad, as it always does. My tapestries argue that. You will be Chief here, and I stand in service to you."

And what did that mean, just? Diarmad tried to remember how the betrothal between Una and Cainnech had come about. Their fathers had been close friends, and maybe the agreement was made in their extreme youth, for it always seemed to have been understood, a given for the future.

Indeed, had the Prince appeared in Scotland just a year later to raise the clans, they would have been already wed, and Una a widow.

Would that have changed anything?

"I fear I can never be the Chief my da was," he said ruefully, "or that Cainnech would ha' been."

"You do no' give yourself enough credit. You never have. Do you ken what Cainnech said about you? That you were a better man with the sword than he and had a heart for justice."

"Och, nay." Yet he had survived the battle while Cainnech had not. As for his heart—did justice lie in aught he had done? From the first his heart had protested the service into which his father pressed him, and he seemed to weigh his honor on a far different scale.

Cainnech had been meant to play the part of the Prince—had apparently agreed to it beforehand, a thing he, Diarmad, never would have done.

"Och, aye," Una returned. "He was so pleased at the man you have become. And I am sure it comforted him at the last to think of you returning home and taking up the place of Chief here, with all its obligations."

Diarmad once more met her gaze. "All of them?"

She gave a small smile. "Let us speak honestly together, Diarmad, as needs must. I know what you are asking, and I assure you, my hand is yours if you want it. My father betrothed me to the next Chief of Clan Ramsay. And…I am not loath."

Shock poured through Diarmad, and his heart protested. Where was her grief now? Where her love for Cainnech, that she could so meekly accept such a substitution?

Was it possible she had always wanted him, Diarmad, after all? It seemed almost sacrilegious to believe she could choose him over Cainnech, yet what else was he to think?

What did he see in her eyes? Nothing, beyond a hint of sorrow. No rage against fate, no passion for Cainnech or himself. No love.

Diarmad drew a ragged breath. "I appreciate your…your fealty," he faltered, "but there is no need to think of such things yet."

"Ah, but I believe there is. You are now the last of your line. You need to beget an heir as soon as ever may be."

And was that the only thing that mattered, begetting an heir? But should that not be done in love and desire? Una offered him neither, just duty wrapped in some fascination with the future and the past.

He thought about Mara arching her body into his as he came to her and gave her his seed—claiming him, holding him. A new thought appeared in his mind: what if Mara carried his child even as the landlady at the Horns of the Moon had believed? Was it not possible, given the wild abandon with which they had made love?

His heart stuttered in his chest. Would she leave him if she knew? But perhaps she did not know yet.

He tried to imagine such a child, fiery-haired and with its mother's courage. His heart stuttered again.

How could he think about begetting an heir on this calm, passionless woman when he wanted Mara MacIvor beneath him? Yet he had always longed for Una. Now she came to him in honor bound.

Gently, he said to Una, "I am glad to know you are not averse. But I feel 'tis much too soon to make such a decision."

"And I say there is no decision to be made. I think we should be wed at once. It will strengthen and reassure the clan."

Did his success as Chief rest with him completing Cainnech's marriage vows? Must he become Cainnech and live the rest of his days so? Aye, he had a duty here, and his father had taught that duty came before all.

But what of his heart? He knew without doubt it did not lie in the grasp of this woman but out on the hillside, in possession of the woman preparing to leave him.

Chapter Thirty-Two

"Mara."

Standing in the twilight with the soft, late dark all around her, Mara heard Diarmad call and thought it a dream. For his was the one—the only—voice she wished to hear before retiring to her bed.

Tomorrow she would arise, take up her few belongings, and away to the south, turning her back on everything her heart desired.

For his sake.

She had steeled herself to ride away without seeing him again. She'd arranged with the kindly Gregor to collect her horse early and avoid all contact. For she had seen Diarmad Ramsay heading for the room in the Chief's house where Una and her women gathered, and she knew what he meant to say. Facing him again would be too much for her to bear.

Already her heart lay shredded in her breast. But she turned toward him anyway, helpless to prevent herself.

He stood half bathed in shadow, a vision all pricked out in black and silver. Aye, surely a dream, for she had longed to see him one more time—to kiss him one more time—solace to carry away with her.

"Ramsay," she said, fighting to keep from revealing her emotion. "I was just making for my bed." *Come there with me, love me once more to last me through eternity*. But she could not say that, for surely he now stood before her betrothed to another. He might believe her a hoyden and a hopelessly wild harridan, as the Sassenach Dwight had implied, but she did retain some shreds of honor.

He reached out as if he would catch hold of her arm, and all her senses anticipated his touch with a mad craving. But he drew his fingers back before they met her flesh.

"Must you go so soon?"

"We have spoken of this. You do no' need me here while you take up a new life."

"So you will just melt away into the mist? Am I never to see you again?"

Pain rushed at Mara, so intense she had to close her eyes a moment. In an effort to fight against it, she said, "She is gey beautiful, your Una. We spoke of this earlier also; not long after we met you told me you had always wanted her. So out of all the grief and terror, something good has come."

Ramsay said nothing.

"Have you spoken to her as I bade you?"

"I have. It seems you were right, she is willing to take me in Cainnech's place."

"Of course she is."

"But I—" He broke off abruptly and made a helpless gesture with his hands.

Mara's heart writhed in sudden hope before crashing to her feet again.

"What is it?" she whispered.

"I hardly know how to ask what I must."

"Speak, Ramsay. After all we ha' been through together"—and all they had done...her mouth cradling him, his tongue stroking her in the most intimate of places—"surely we do not fear a few words."

He gave a low, rueful laugh that chased a shiver up Mara's spine. "From the first, Mara MacIvor, your courage has shamed me. You are a woman in a thousand, nay, ten thousand."

Heat flushed Mara's cheeks. "I ken fine what I am." Not a patch on that beautiful, regal woman in the Chief's house, and certainly not worthy of this man.

"Culloden," she said, "tore the fabric of this country apart and many lives with it, including yours and mine. When your father laid his duty on you, you wanted not the task. And you wanted not me in your life, Diarmad Ramsay. I am an unwelcome complication, but I will remove myself so you might heal as best you may."

"Not before I ask what I must."

"Then ask it!"

"When I met wi' her today, Una spoke of the necessity of begetting an heir as soon as possible."

Of course she had. Even Una could not be so bloodless as to mislike the prospect of this man between her legs. But Mara said nothing, her throat suddenly too tight.

Ramsay stumbled on, "And I thought—that is, I could no' but wonder... All those times I came to you, and the landlady's assumption in Ullapool... Surely 'tis possible you already carry my child."

Was it? Aye, and Mara had contemplated the question before, the possibility so bright it made her dizzy. The truth was, she did not know. Only time would tell.

"And," she said carefully, "if I do?"

"Then you cannot leave." He captured her hands in his, and warmth enfolded her. "'Twould change everything."

Would it? Would a bairn—his bairn—in her belly change the woman she was, make her acceptable to him?

A second thought followed hard on the first: she could lie, claim that aye, she carried the seed of his house—the future of Clan Ramsay—and stay here with him. They would lie together again, and if it were not already true, it soon would be.

But could she begin her future with this man, whom she valued more than her own life, on a lie?

She shook her head.

His fingers tightened on hers. "Nay? You say you do no' carry my child?"

"Una is the woman for you," she said. "Not me." Una, whom he had always desired; Una, who made a fit match for him. This did not make too great a sacrifice on Mara's part for the man she loved.

He stiffened. "Is this about what you think o' me, Mara MacIvor?"

"What I think o' you?"

As if he forced the words, he said, "I sensed how your feelings for me changed after I abandoned the task laid upon me. Aye, I ken you have said a greater duty lies here for me now. But it occurs to me those might be words one friend speaks to another."

"Aye, for that is what we are. Friends." *And lovers. Your tongue sliding over my skin, claiming me completely.*

"I hope so."

"Let me go, Ramsay." Deliberately, she drew her

hands from his. "My leaving has naught to do wi' what I may think of you." *And all to do wi' what you think of me.*

"I canno' let you go if you carry my child."

But, Mara's heart protested, *I want you to want me, not just your child.*

"Do not fash yourself. I will leave in the morning."

"Mara, please."

Say you love me, she bade him silently. *Tell me that for all my faults you cannot live without me and will accept me, heedless and shameless as I may be.*

But he just stood there silent in the darkness, and Mara turned from him and without answer carried her broken heart away to her solitary bed.

****

"Soldiers—soldiers!" Eamon, breathless, came running and hollering the words as he ran. "Chief Diarmad, I saw them from the top of the rise. A whole troop of men!"

Diarmad froze where he stood, caught in the full light of morning with Una at his side. She had trapped him in conversation as he headed out to find Mara MacIvor, determined to keep her from departing even if he had to beg. Yet if she now despised him for his loss of honor, how could he constrain her to stay?

The endless night just behind him had held such torment, imagining a future that stretched before him devoid of her presence, almost anything seemed better. But not this.

Eamon, eyes wide, reached his side, and Diarmad caught the lad's shoulders to steady him.

"What, now? English soldiers?"

"I do no' ken—I could no' see. But the sun

glittered off their weapons."

"How many?"

Eamon shook his head helplessly. "Half a score?" he guessed.

"Run, get my sword."

"Diarmad, no." Una, still beside him, laid her hand on his arm. "If they are English soldiers, you cannot be found armed—you will be seized and deported, or worse."

Rage rose to Diarmad's head. She was right, curse it. But was he to stand by while his home and his people were threatened? They might just as well take a Highlander's balls as his weapons.

"We do no' ken 'tis the English," he snapped. How could it be? Why would a troop of English soldiers follow him here? For followed he must have been. By Dwight? But the man had let him and Mara go; it made no sense.

Gregor appeared beside him, concern etched on his craggy face. "Trouble?"

"Och, aye. Round up what men and weapons you can."

"Diarmad," Una objected again.

He turned on her. "You canno' expect me to meet a lot of invaders wi'out a sword in my hand." More kindly he added, "Go inside; gather the women and keep them safe. We do no' ken what is coming."

Una paled. "You think we women could be attacked?"

"If these who approach be enemy and if we defenders fall," he told her baldly, "I would no' like to think what will happen."

She spun in a swirl of black hair and went inside.

Seumas stumped up, balanced perilously on his two sticks.

"I heard. The rest of the men are on their way—few as we may be."

Diarmad met the gaze of his friend. "Go you in and guard the women—Una gathers them even now."

"Nay, but—"

"Seumas, I do no' doubt your courage. You ha' the heart of a hawk." Diarmad examined his friend, barely healed from dire injuries. "But I need you there."

"Aye, Chief," Seumas answered, making it clear he obeyed against his will, and took it as an official order.

"Before you go"—Diarmad stayed him a precious moment even as Eamon, now accompanied by several other lads, came bearing weapons—"Ha' you seen Mara MacIvor?"

Seumas shook his head.

Eamon spoke up. "Was no' Mistress MacIvor to leave this morn? She asked Gregor to have her pony ready."

"And did he?" Diarmad speared him with a look.

"I am no' certain; I ha' not seen her. She may ha' ridden out on her own." The lad cast a desperate glance toward the rise. "You ken what she is like."

Diarmad did: hasty, reckless, fearless—the woman who ruled his heart.

Why had he failed to realize that sooner? Mara with her wild hair and those eyes so full of emotion, he could no more live without her than without breath.

But he had no chance to search for her now. For he could see them coming down the slope of the glen at a fast trot.

Not a troop of soldiers, nay—this bunch came in

ragged formation and wore no uniforms. Even as Diarmad raised his sword, they broke into a wild yell and the figure at their head...

Diarmad narrowed his eyes and stepped forward with what few men he had at his back. He would meet the first rush as he must—and die here on this beloved ground if he had to, on this bonny morning.

Aye, for bonny it was; the sun, just risen, caught the flaming head of the man who came first, riding his mount heavily and clad in an assortment of shabby plaids.

"False Prince," Archibald bellowed as he drew up his horse and swung his sword for Diarmad's head. "Do ye remember me?"

Chapter Thirty-Three

Mara MacIvor, already astride her mount and ready to ride out, heard a great yell that sounded as if torn from many throats, and her blood turned cold in her veins. She had waited long at the pony shed for old Gregor, and when he failed to appear had led her pony out and loaded him with her few possessions—little more than a blanket and a single bundle of ragged clothing.

But the cries that now split the air had her head up much like that of the pony. She'd not heard anything like since the battle in the Horns of the Moon tavern, and terror pierced her heart.

What horror could it be, here in this peaceful place?

The pony shed lay some distance behind the Chief's house. She urged her mount out around the big, stone building and saw...

At first her eyes refused to accept the evidence before them. She blinked and squinted against the morning light. A horde of armed, mounted men rushed a smaller group who stood out before the settlement. Even as she watched she saw the foremost of the footmen raise his sword to meet the onslaught, his hair gleaming bright in the sun.

Ramsay.

Her poor heart faltered in her breast. But this could

not be what it seemed. How could attackers find him here? And who were they? Even as she urged her mount forward, using her knees because her hands were already busy drawing her weapon, she recognized the brute who rode in upon Diarmad, and she cursed loudly.

Archibald!

It seemed not just MacNeal had survived the conflict between him and the bandit laird. And even though MacNeal now lay in the hands of English soldiers, Archibald must have followed her and Ramsay over all that rough country and come looking for vengeance.

Her mind fumbled with it even as her mount sped forward, hell bent. Diarmad's clan had been decimated; he now stood with but a few men—wounded, elders, and mere lads.

Even as she rode up she heard Archibald bellow, "I will ha' your head, man! Not so much the monarch now, are ye?"

Ramsay did not bother to reply. Hair flying, he spun as Archibald's horse drove in on him, striving to meet every thrust of Archibald's blade with his own. But his position on foot against a throng of mounted men put him, like his warriors, at a sore disadvantage. Even before Mara reached him, she saw Archibald's blade miss his head by a mere hair.

"Archibald!" she called.

Men hollered, cried, and fell all around her, and the big brute did not hear. Incredibly, Ramsay did, and his expression—set and grim—altered to wild dismay.

"Mara, go back!"

That moment of distraction cost him dear.

Archibald's blade swung again and Ramsay went down on one knee.

Struck? Mara could not tell, but her fear had her pushing her mount forward, bent on maneuvering between the two men.

"You!" Archibald's countenance, as red as his hair, had become a mask of hate. In the midst of the wild melee he fixed his maddened gaze upon Mara and spat, "I'll ha' you now, wench—one way or t'other."

Stand steady, Mara beseeched her mount silently even as she raised her weapon—no sword for her, but only a long knife. She ducked as Archibald's deadly blade swooped at her, seeking blood, and she struck like an adder with the knife. An unfair fight, aye, but she could at least hope to bleed and weaken the brute.

"Mara!" Ramsay bellowed, and her heart strengthened within her. *He lives.*

Relief brought tears to her eyes and blurred Archibald's ugly visage. The bright blade swooped once more and caught the flesh of her arm. She did not even feel the pain. Neither did she experience fear: all her emotion centered on the man behind her. Her life was his, and if she had to spend her last drop of blood on his behalf, she would and gladly.

She could still hear him bellowing like a man gone mad. All around, his warriors fell—but so, too, did those in Archibald's train. Mara felt each one of them drop even though her gaze remained fused to Archibald's. She could feel Ramsay's emotions, as well, but one thought obsessed her mind.

Ramsay must not fall.

Even as the words screamed through her mind, Archibald swung his sword again. Mara ducked beneath the shining blade, knife at the ready, and plunged her smaller blade into the brute's heart.

Time froze for an instant as Archibald's sword, still falling, completed its arc. Mara felt the blade strike the back of her neck like a razor-edged stone, and as Archibald slid from his mount, she fell also, her mind shrieking in dismay.

The great clamor around her went abruptly silent as she tumbled into the green grass. She had one glimpse of Ramsay's face above her, twisted in agony, and thought, *Good. He will be the last thing I see and a sight to carry to eternity.* The darkness reached out to meet her, and even though she did not want to, though she longed to stay instead with him, she surrendered.

****

"Well, Mara, and did I no' tell you your haste and heedlessness would one day cost you dearly?"

Mara turned her head in surprise at the sound of her mother's voice. Rhiannan MacIvor stood not far away, hands busy at a job she had always loved, dying threads. Mara's gaze moved from the skeins of wool already hung drying in the gorse bushes to the great pot that had stained her mother's hands. Red. All the thread was red as blood.

"Ma," Mara said on a rush of impossible gladness. "How is it you are here?" Her mother had been killed along with Janet. Yet she appeared much as she always had, her reddish hair caught back in a riot of curls, her complexion smooth and flawless, and her eyes serene blue. Nay—she appeared better than she had, all the small lines lent by care flown.

Rhiannan directed a look at her daughter, both fond and appraising. "Do you no' mean, how is it you are here?"

Mara glanced around. They were, in fact, on the green sward in front of their shieling, which still stood intact as it had most her life—not burned. Or were they?

"Where are we?" she asked, a chill pricking her spine.

"Where do you suppose?"

"Dead." Mara raised a tentative hand to the back of her neck, seeking the place where Archibald's blade had kissed her just below the skull. The flesh there felt whole.

Her mother smiled. "Foolish lass. You ever were one to give your heart first and think of the consequences later. Just so did you give your heart to your prince."

"Charlie?" Mara considered it. From the distance lent by this far, quiet place, she could see things so much more clearly. "Surely he was worthy? He *is* Scotland, and if I do no' live—and die—for Scotland, then for what?"

"That is your father speaking, and no mistake." The smile in Rhiannan's eyes deepened. "And you may look at it so, if you will. But I did not mean Charles Edward." Her gaze met Mara's. "I speak of *your* prince—he who has laid claim to your heart."

"Ramsay." Just speaking his name made Mara quiver with longing. "He is done with me. Like you, Ma, he knows me for wild and wayward—he will choose a woman like Una, whom he has always loved, and who possesses a measure of decorum."

"Will he?" Rhiannan plunged her hands back into the vat of red liquid.

"Aye, for back in Ullapool I was exposed and denounced for what I am. Willful. Crude. His attitude toward me changed then."

"So why does he grieve for you so deeply now?"

"What?"

"Do you no' hear him?" Rhiannan cocked her head like a woman listening. "He pours out his sorrow for you as if his heart has burst."

Mara listened but could hear nothing save a gentle breeze over the green sward. She demanded, "Can you truly hear anything beyond this place?"

Her mother returned, "I have waited here and listened hard. 'Tis possible, while those we love still remain in the world."

Mara shivered with a trace of chill. "So this truly is the afterlife. If so, where is Janet?"

Rhiannan's clear, blue eyes met Mara's. "She has moved on."

"Eh?"

"Aye, Daughter. Janet examined her life, a thing everyone who comes here must do, and decided she had no' lived fully enough before she died. In truth she wished she had been more like you."

"Me!"

"Aye—courageous and valiant, so she said— throwing her heart at things and no' wasting time in doubt or fear. For, as she learned once she viewed her past, a careful life brings little but regret. She has passed through the cauldron," Rhiannon gestured to the pot full of red in which her hands rested, "and now embarks on a new life, which she vows to live differently."

"But I have regrets also, Ma. I regret that I was no'

the woman Ramsay wanted me to be. That I will never see him or hold him again—that I did no' tell him what he means to me when I had the chance."

Rhiannan smiled kindly. "Then, Daughter, go to him."

"How?"

"This is a waiting place, not a stopping place, Mara. It is a place of peace where one studies one's heart and goes on—or sometimes goes back."

"Can I go back to him?"

"If you have the courage, and if you want it enough. If you can hear him calling you. Listen."

Mara did, using not her senses this time but her whole being. At first she heard but that gentle wind, the only thing to disturb the beautiful silence that surrounded them. She could not hear even the beat of her own heart. Then, faint and distant, she caught a sliver of sound—the voice that meant all the world to her.

She felt the pull then, as if upon a tie wrapped around her heart and binding her to Diarmad Ramsay, one unbroken even in death.

Gladness and sorrow arose in a staggering wave. She did not want to leave her mother. She knew, also, she returned to pain and the bright, noisy perils of the world.

But no fear or dread could overset what she felt for Diarmad Ramsay. He spoke her name, and by love she was bound.

Chapter Thirty-Four

"Mara, lass. Mara, for the love of God, do no' leave me!"

"Diarmad, Diarmad, she is already gone."

Diarmad, only partially aware that Seumas had lowered himself painfully beside the place where Mara MacIvor lay, disregarded him. He knelt in the grass which bore bright crimson splashes of blood—Mara MacIvor's blood—and tears burned down his face. They could not be his tears, for he rarely wept—barely for his father and not at all for Cainnech. But now his heart had burst and darkness rushed out, sharp as pain.

Mara MacIvor, eyes closed, lay on her back, cradled between his hands. Her hair made a splash of color nearly as bright as the red blood, but all life had flown her pale face. Where her courage now, that which had led her to attack Archibald? Where the strong will that had moved her, the great surging life that had met him every time he looked into her eyes?

"No," he said and felt Seumas place a hand on his shoulder. "Did you no' see her?" he demanded in the voice of a shattered man. "Did you see her rush in? Did you see her fight for me?"

"Aye," Seumas said softly. "The heart o' a lion. She turned the fight, lad, and won the day. Let us gather her up now. We will bury her with honor as she deserves."

"Nay!" Unheeding, Diarmad drew Mara into his arms, close against his heart. The wound at the back of her neck still oozed blood, and he pressed his fingers to it as if he could make her whole again, barely aware that his folk stood about him among their slain attackers, staring and speechless.

"I canno'," he cried. "I canno' go on without her, not for one day."

Someone dropped to the grass at his other side. He caught a glimpse of long, dark hair and turned to look into Una's eyes.

For once—the first time Diarmad could recall—they brimmed with emotion, no longer misty and mysterious; a real woman looked out at him.

"You love her. Diarmad, why did you no' say?"

"Duty. It lay here," he managed to croak out. None of that mattered now, not a whit. All that mattered was the passion in Mara MacIvor's soul and the way she made him feel.

"Aye, so," Una said softly, "but love is a duty as well—one of the heart." Diarmad felt rather than saw her exchange a look with Seumas, at his other side.

"If you love her, call her," Una urged him.

"But she is gone."

"Love hears, sees, and answers far beyond this world and, I believe, even into the next. Call her. Call her with your heart."

Diarmad closed his eyes and felt for the bright spirit that had come to mean everything to him.

"Mara. Mara, lass. Mara—my love."

No answer. His hand, curled around Mara's throat, felt no pulse, no indrawn breath.

Mara, he called not with his voice but his spirit,

soul to soul. *I canno' live without you. Have mercy on me!*

She jerked in his arms. Faint, so faint beneath her skin, his fingers felt a heartbeat—that which he now knew drove his world. Broken and remade, he bent his head.

****

"Archibald is dead? Are you certain?"

Still disoriented, Mara lay upon a pallet in a quiet chamber. A heavy bandage swathed her neck, and Diarmad's face hovered above her—all she truly wished to see. His hand clasped her fingers, and she could feel his emotions battering at her even though she could not quite define them all.

"Dead he is, and the rest of his men slain or flown. 'Twas you killed him, lass. That knife of yours went straight into his ugly heart. Do you no' recall?"

"I am no longer sure what is real and what imagined. I was with my mother, Diarmad. She bade me return to you."

His fingers tightened on hers painfully. "Bless her for it."

"I was no' certain you would want me back." Though she almost believed, given the way he now looked at her, that he had.

"Not want you?" He threaded his fingers through hers. Aye, and that was how she wanted to spend the rest of her life—entwined with him. But what of the distance that had existed between them since Ullapool?

Before she could ask, he bent his head over their joined hands.

"Mara, 'tis I who doubted you wanted me, even as I rued the loss of your regard. I ken fine I am no' the

241

man you might wish me to be."

"Eh?" Her eyes went wide; he could not be more the man she wished if she had created him from a mound of clay. She adored every separate thing about him, from those handsome gray-blue eyes to the scruff on his chin, every hair, every freckle.

He visibly wrestled some emotion. "My honor is tainted. And I felt how you changed toward me after I broke faith with my promise to aid the Prince. But—"

Mara drew breath and interrupted him. "Me, change? 'Twas you who went off me, once you had it pointed out by that Sassenach, Dwight, back in Ullapool, what a terrible wild and undisciplined sort of woman I am."

He blinked at her; she tightened her fingers on his and went on speaking. "I am that sorry to tell you this, Ramsay, but I fear I will never change. I would like to, for your sake. Aye, and I would do most aught I could to make you happy, but my heedlessness seems bred in my bones. And I am afraid I am no' the woman to live a lie."

"Thank God." His smile flashed at her, and against all the odds her heart rose. Strange, how her well-being could rest on this man's smile, on the light in his eyes; astonishing, that her future could rest on the gift of his company. "Mara, lass—beautiful Mara, Mara my love—I never condemned you. I thought you had condemned me! You were so determined to hold to the honor of that promise by which we were bound…"

Mara gazed into his eyes, and her poor heart, which seemed to have endured so much, settled into a steady rhythm. Half disbelieving, she asked, "You never despised me?"

"Nor you, me?"

She shook her head. "The sun of my world rises and sets on you, Diarmad Ramsay."

"And mine is carried on the strength of your bonny spirit, Mara MacIvor." He bent down and kissed her, and the sweetness of it banished all doubt.

Thank you, Ma, she said silently. *I will see you anon. For now, I ha' a life to live.*

As if to confirm it, Diarmad lifted his lips from hers—not far—and bade, "Wed wi' me?"

A rush of sheer bliss made it impossible for Mara to speak. Then reality crept in. "What of Una?"

"Una?" he repeated as if he had never heard the name.

"Does she no' consider herself betrothed to you?"

"Well, now, that is a curious thing. I had a chance to speak with Una not long before you woke. It seems she is, and has always been, in love wi' Seumas."

"Seumas!" Mara repeated it in astonishment. "Why did she never say?"

"Because she'd been pledged as future wife to the Chief's house by her father long before she was grown. Like me, she felt herself honor bound." Diarmad's eyes held Mara's, and she felt his love, steady and strong. "But since my honor is already broken, I have freed her from that obligation. Seumas nearly died at Culloden. Let her have her love, as I will have mine. Aye?" Desire flared in his eyes. "Do I have mine, Mara? Will you wed wi' me?"

But she had one thing to say before giving him any such promise. "Your honor, Diarmad Ramsay, is no' broken. It seems clear there are bonds even stronger than the promise you gave your father—like those laid by your heart."

"Love," he whispered.

"Love," she agreed, and warmth enfolded her; the brightness in his eyes now consumed all doubt.

"Tell me you love me, Mara MacIvor. Say it out loud, with all the strength of your spirit."

"I love you, Diarmad Ramsay, with my whole being and every drop of my blood."

"It is well, for I love you so much it half terrifies me." His lips hovered above hers. "Say you will wed wi' me," he begged for the third time, "so I might go on breathing."

And mercifully Mara did.

A word about the author...

Born and raised in Western New York, multi-published Laura Strickland has been an avid reader and writer since childhood. Embracing her mother's heritage, she has pursued a lifelong interest in Celtic lore, legend, and music, all reflected in her writing.

While she loves to travel, she is usually happiest at home, not far from Lake Ontario, with her husband and her "fur child," a rescue dog.

Her other Scottish romances include *Devil Black* and *His Wicked Highland Ways*.